VICTORIAN
MANSION
FLOWER SHOP
MYSTERIES

A Seedy Development

Elizabeth Penney

AnniesFiction.com

Books in the Victorian Mansion
Flower Shop Mysteries series

Library of Congress-in-Publication Data
A Seedy Development / by Elizabeth Penney
p. cm.
I. Title
2018965126

AnniesFiction.com
(800) 282-6643
Victorian Mansion Flower Shop Mysteries™
Series Creators: Shari Lohner, Janice Tate
Editor: Elizabeth Morrissey
Cover Illustrator: Bob Kayganich

10 11 12 13 14 | Printed in South Korea | 9 8 7 6 5 4 3

1

When an airport tower became visible above the trees lining the forested road, Kaylee Bleu raised her eyebrows in surprise. "I never knew there was an airport out this way," she said to her friend and shop assistant, Mary Bishop, who sat in the passenger seat of Kaylee's SUV. "Seeing is believing, I guess."

"The Turtle Cove Airport is the smallest airport in the San Juan Islands, but it's active," Mary replied, then gestured backward over her shoulder. "Looks like Bear is excited."

Kaylee glanced in the rearview mirror at the dachshund riding in the back seat, his nose pressed to the window, and she chuckled. "Bear loves airports. They're another place for him to explore and meet new people."

Mary pointed to a large sign depicting the silhouette of an airplane and the name of the airfield. "Take the next right."

As Kaylee slowed to turn, she scanned another sign just past the first one that listed various flying businesses located at the airport. She spotted a shipping service, helicopter scenic tours, and something called an FBO.

"What's an FBO?" she asked. "And actually, I'm not totally sure what a fly-in is either." She and Mary were headed to a meeting for vendors participating in Orcas Island, Washington's, Apple Fest Fly-In, a fall-themed event to be held on the airport grounds. The Flower Patch, the business Kaylee had purchased from her grandmother, was going to host a booth at the multiday event.

"An FBO is a fixed-base operation providing services to pilots," Mary explained. "Like fuel, repairs, and tie-downs."

"Tie-downs? You mean they secure parked planes with lines to keep them in place?"

"That's as good a description as any."

"You sure know the lingo," Kaylee said.

Amusement sparkled in Mary's eyes. "I wouldn't know it if my darling husband hadn't bought me a glider ride for my sixtieth birthday."

Kaylee laughed. "Herb sure knows the way to your heart."

"He does still surprise me sometimes, even after all these years," Mary said. "As for your other question, a fly-in is when pilots bring their planes to a certain location for a get-together."

"That's a unique idea." Kaylee navigated her Ford Escape along the winding approach road. "I read in the paper that antique, military, and experimental planes will be exhibited."

Mary nodded. "There's one now."

To their left, a red biplane of World War I-era vintage was taxiing along the runway. A moment later, the aircraft lifted off and soon became a bright dot in the clear blue sky.

Kaylee brought her gaze back to earth to focus on her destination, a cluster of metal buildings ahead. "Oh good. Jess and DeeDee are here," she observed when she saw their vehicles among the others in the parking lot. Along with Mary and Kaylee, Jessica Roberts and DeeDee Wilcox rounded out the Petal Pushers garden club.

For the Apple Fest, Jessica and DeeDee were sharing Kaylee's booth to sell items related to their own businesses. While Kaylee planned to offer wreaths and other decorations from her flower shop, Jessica would bring loads of delicious treats from her bakery, Death by Chocolate, which sat beside The Flower Patch on Turtle Cove's Main Street. DeeDee would be selling her handmade goat milk soap as well as any apple- or flying-themed books she had in stock at her mystery bookstore, Between the Lines, another Main Street business.

As Kaylee pulled into the parking area, she caught sight of an orchard with heavily laden trees beyond a tall mesh fence at the end of the lot. Considering the orchard's close proximity to the airport and the apple theme of the fest, she wondered if the orchard owner was involved with the event.

Kaylee slid her SUV into a spot at the end of the lot next to a shiny black pickup she recognized instantly as belonging to the island's most popular handyman, Reese Holt. Her pulse ratcheted up a tiny bit at the thought of seeing her handsome friend.

"This is a good turnout," Mary said. "The Turtle Cove Festivities Committee must have done a great job getting the word out."

"I'm not surprised," Kaylee said. "They always bring their A game when they're prepping for special events."

Mary unlatched her seat belt and picked up her purse. "The Apple Fest is a little outside their purview, but hopefully it'll bring lots of visitors to town."

"The more the merrier," Kaylee said, then climbed out and went to the back to clip Bear's leash to his collar. He hopped out of the car and started trotting toward a pair of double doors on the closest building, clearly assuming that Kaylee and Mary would come along.

A sign beside the propped-open doors denoted the building as the Turtle Cove FBO. The sound of voices drifted out, but the muffled noise was soon overpowered by a throaty rumble coming from the parking lot.

Kaylee stopped and turned toward the source of the roar. A huge, red diesel pickup barreled between lines of parked cars right toward her and Bear.

Kaylee prepared to scoop up her dog and leap out of the way, but the truck screeched to a halt a few feet away from her.

The driver's side window was rolled down, revealing a scowling blonde woman in a lime-green windbreaker at the wheel. The passenger side door opened, and a short, stout man wearing khakis and a polo shirt slid down.

"Don't bother to pick me up," he said, an English accent flavoring his words. "I'll catch a ride with Brett." He slammed the door.

Leaning out of her open window, the woman yelled at him, "I'm calling my lawyer tomorrow!"

The man flapped a hand and stomped along the pavement. Under one arm, he carried a leather portfolio. The truck roared off, looping back onto the road with a squeal of tires. The diesel engine's grumble receded into the distance.

"Wasn't that nice?" Mary muttered as she and Kaylee started walking again, eager to distance themselves from the feuding couple.

When the man caught up with them near the entrance, Kaylee did her best to pretend she hadn't heard a thing. "Good evening," she said when it became apparent not greeting him would be rude.

"Evening," he replied with a short nod. He stood back to let them enter the building first, then brushed past them as they walked into a large room full of people.

Rows of folding chairs were set up in the middle of the space, which had big picture windows viewing the runway. Two long tables were set up to one side, offering drinks and plates of cookies. A young man with frizzy hair and a petite, older woman with pale, permed curls lingered near a podium at the front of the room, apparently waiting for the meeting to begin. The man from the parking lot joined them.

Kaylee glanced around. Closed doors marked *Office* and *Restrooms* led off the main room, and a kitchenette was located in an alcove, but that appeared to be the extent of the place. Although his truck was parked outside, Reese was nowhere to be seen.

"Kaylee, Mary, over here. We saved your seats." Jessica waved from a chair in the middle row. Beside her, DeeDee smiled and lifted a paper cup, indicating that they should get themselves some refreshments. Their purses rested on two adjacent chairs. Most of the other seats were full or reserved with a coat or bag.

"Want something to drink?" Mary asked. "I think I'd like a coffee."

"That sounds good." Kaylee followed Mary to the table, where they availed themselves of coffee and chocolate oatmeal cookies.

"Mmmm. I can tell who made these cookies," Mary said, nodding toward Jessica.

"Jess's touch is unmistakable," Kaylee agreed.

The duo edged their way through the chairs, Bear trotting along behind them. People paused their visiting to greet the adorable dog, who wore a bow tie with a parachute print. Bear had an ever-growing collection of bow ties to suit any occasion, and they made excellent conversation starters.

"Thanks for saving us a place," Kaylee said as she and Mary settled beside DeeDee. Bear sat on the floor, lifting his snout in hopes of dropped crumbs. Not wanting him to feel left out, Kaylee found a biscuit in her bag for him.

"You made it just in time." DeeDee nodded toward the clock on the wall, which indicated it was a few minutes past the hour.

Kaylee sipped her coffee and delighted in the rich flavor. "Did Jess bring the coffee too?"

Jessica leaned forward so she could see Kaylee across DeeDee. "Sure did. If you'd ever tasted the coffee the manager here makes, you'd thank me."

"Did you notice the organic apple orchard next door?" DeeDee asked. "It belongs to my godfather, Wilfred Bates. He's also a pilot and airplane mechanic."

"That's handy," Kaylee said. "Being right next door to the airport."

DeeDee scowled. "Yes, unfortunately other people think that too. They've been—"

"Good evening, ladies and gentlemen." The frizzy-haired man at the front of the room had stepped forward to the podium. "I'm Brett Horne, airport manager, and I'd like to welcome you to our humble operation." His smug smile belied his modest words. "Tonight we're going to discuss the upcoming Apple Fest Fly-In, specifically vendor placement and rules." He gestured to the petite, older woman. "I'll let Lorraine Swift here tell you all about it."

DeeDee whispered to Kaylee, "That's Wilfred's lady friend. She's been trying to pin him down for years." She nodded toward a burly young man in the front row wearing a ball cap. "And that's her son, Floyd."

Lorraine smiled wanly at the group as she bustled to the podium. She pulled the microphone down to where she could easily speak into it. "Hello. It's good to see you all. The first annual Apple Fest Fly-In is sure to be a big success with your help."

The sound of an airplane engine grew louder, the motor whining as the craft approached. The audience turned toward the big windows, curious to see what was coming in. Lorraine said another couple of words, something about sign-ups, but gave up once she saw she'd lost her listeners.

A small red-and-white plane taxied along the paved strip, coming to a smooth stop right in front of the building. A door over one wing opened, and two men climbed out. One was older, rangy, and lean, wearing a ball cap. The other was Reese Holt.

"Wilfred gives lessons too," DeeDee said. "He's a flight instructor."

Kaylee sat back against the hard chair, amazed. She'd seen Reese only yesterday, and he hadn't said a thing about learning to fly.

"Now that you two are here," Lorraine said as instructor and student entered the room, "we can continue."

"Quite an entrance, guys," the shorter, older man at the front of the room cracked. "Should have thought of it myself."

Better than being dropped off by an angry woman, Kaylee thought.

"Yeah, your Beech 18 would have upstaged us for sure, David," Wilfred said, finding a seat in the front row. Reese sat in another vacant seat a few places down.

David nodded in acknowledgment, then returned his attention to Lorraine, who gave the microphone another adjustment. "Let's move on," she said.

Lorraine droned on about vendor paperwork, then answered questions from the audience while passing out a series of forms. After she wrapped up her portion, David took the helm. Kaylee shoved the pile of paper handouts into her bag, thinking that later would be soon enough to go over it all.

"Hi, I'm David Smythe." He spelled his last name for them. "I'm the leading pilot based at this airport."

DeeDee gave a soft snort. "I thought that was Wilfred."

"I won't keep you long," David went on, "but I wanted to let you know about the planes that we've got coming." He clicked a remote and a slideshow began playing on a screen behind the podium. The impressive roster featured retired military bombers, helicopters, and ultralight airplanes. "We have pilots coming from ten states so far," David said, then clicked one more time, revealing what looked like a property map divided into lots.

"Did he have to go there?" DeeDee hissed under her breath.

Kaylee glanced over to see her friend scowling, an expression not frequently seen on the cheerful bookshop owner.

Lorraine stepped forward. "Is this really the best time?" She sent a glance toward the front row, where Wilfred sat.

"It's all right, Lorraine," Brett said. "I told him he could make the announcement."

She subsided and stood near the wall, but her arms were crossed, and she glared at David.

"This is a map of a proposed fly-in community," David announced. "The planning board has given us preliminary approval to create half a dozen house lots on land I own adjacent to the airport."

"What's a fly-in community?" someone called.

"Glad you asked. A fly-in community is built adjacent to a small airport. It includes houses and hangars so pilots can literally walk out their front doors and hop into their airplanes." David smiled. "This project will bring a lot of tax revenue to the island and increase business at this airport. All good things for property owners."

There were more questions, while DeeDee fumed the entire time. Kaylee didn't understand her reaction. The fly-in community sounded neat, reminding her of homes with private docks, but using airspace instead of water.

Once the meeting broke up, however, Kaylee learned the answer. As they stood, DeeDee waved to her godfather. "Wilfred. Over here."

Wilfred picked his way through the chairs, followed by Reese, who greeted Kaylee with a smile. "My new student's not doing too badly," Wilfred told them proudly.

Reese laughed. "It's not the flying, it's the landing that worries me. I have to admit I was glad when we touched down."

"You did a good job, Reese." Lorraine appeared at Wilfred's elbow, her son hovering behind her. "Smooth as silk." Much shorter than her beau, she stood on tiptoes to give him a peck on the cheek.

DeeDee introduced her friends to Wilfred, Lorraine, and

Floyd, then took Wilfred's arm. "Wilfred's always been like a second father to me."

The ruggedly handsome older man patted his goddaughter's arm. "And you've been like a daughter to me." He chuckled. "And Polly and Zoe are like my grandchildren."

"You spoil my daughters too much," DeeDee said lightly. "I'm pretty sure they're the only students at the elementary school who've copiloted a scenic plane tour of Orcas Island."

Lorraine, who'd been listening to this exchange with pursed lips, elbowed her way to the center of the group. "Floyd and I operate Deep Green Cleaning." She pressed business cards on Kaylee, Mary, and Jessica. "We do high-end houses and special projects, here on Orcas and via boat to other islands. Please feel free to pass the cards along to anyone who might need us."

Kaylee tucked the card into her bag. "I own The Flower Patch in town. Quite a few of our customers are putting on events. They might need cleaners, so I'll mention you if it comes up."

"I appreciate that." Seeming pleased, Lorraine turned to her son. "You hear that, Floyd? We might have some new customers."

The young man nodded, seeming content to let his more outgoing mother take the social lead.

"I couldn't believe it when David brought up the development tonight," DeeDee said. "You must have been so upset, Wilfred."

Wilfred shook his head. "Not really. Nothing's going to stop them building on his land."

"My husband went to the planning board meetings, and he told me the proposed houses will add a lot to the tax base," Jessica said. Her husband, Luke, was a tax accountant.

"As long as they stop there." Lorraine rolled her eyes.

Mary, sensitive to social cues, changed the subject. "Did I hear that you're helping with the entertainment lineup, Lorraine?"

"I sure am," Lorraine said. "We need more bands for the

entertainment during the closing party on the last night."

"Well, have I got a group for you," Mary said brightly. "My husband, Herb, has been talking to DeeDee and Jess's husbands. They're willing to get together and play a set of classic rock songs."

"Andy agreed?" DeeDee's mouth dropped open. "He hasn't played for . . . well, since Zoe was born." Her smile was reminiscent. "He brought his guitar to the hospital room and played for us."

"Herb is playing guitar too," Mary said. "Luke can play bass. Now they only need a drummer."

"I can handle that," Reese said. "I'm a pretty fair drummer, if I do say so myself."

Kaylee regarded Reese with admiration. She'd learned two new things about him tonight: that he was adventurous enough to learn to fly, and he was musical too. She hung back to talk to him as the others filed out of the room. "How was your lesson?" she asked.

"Awesome." Reese pulled out his wallet and handed Kaylee a plastic card. "This is my student pilot certificate. I even have my own logbook."

"You're all official and everything. Congratulations." She beamed as she handed the card back to him.

"Maybe you can come up with us sometime," Reese said as he slid the card back into his wallet and pocketed it. "You'll be safe, since Wilfred will be there."

Kaylee marveled at the idea of viewing the San Juan Islands from above. "I'd love that."

As they began walking toward the open door to the parking lot, Kaylee heard voices from outside. When a coarse laugh rang out, she slowed instinctively.

"We can do it the hard way or the easy way." Kaylee recognized David Smythe's English accent. "Either way, I'm going to get your land, mate. Count on it."

2

Reese sent Kaylee a concerned frown, but she shrugged it off and started moving again. Outside, Wilfred and David stood near the entrance. The Petal Pushers chatted with Lorraine and Floyd some distance away. By their body language, Kaylee guessed they hadn't heard David's statement. *Or was it a threat?*

"As I've told you before," Wilfred said as Kaylee and Reese emerged, "I'm not interested in selling. My family has been on that land for over a century."

"I'm afraid it's too late." David clapped Wilfred on the shoulder. "The time for negotiation is coming to an end."

As David walked back into the building, Floyd called out, "David. Hold up." The other man barely looked back as Floyd hurried after him.

"Is everything all right?" Kaylee asked Wilfred, who was staring after the English pilot, seemingly lost in thought.

The older man shook his head. "Fine. Everything is fine." He blinked pale blue eyes that warmed when he drew his gaze from the doorway to Kaylee and Reese. "Are you two coming over to the farm? DeeDee wants me to show you around the orchard."

Kaylee glanced at Mary and her other friends. "I'd love to, but I need to check with Mary. She's riding with me."

Mary agreed enthusiastically to the detour so Kaylee drove over to the farm, which was reached via a lane a short distance down the road that went back toward Turtle Cove. Kaylee had been so intent on finding the airport she hadn't noticed the painted sign, which read:

Bates Fruit Farm
From our family to yours since 1890.

"I've seen their fruit in the supermarket," Mary said. "They grow peaches, cherries, and plums as well as apples."

"Now that you mention it, I have too," Kaylee said. "I recognize the logo."

They navigated along a narrow road between rows of fruit trees with distinctive twisted shapes. To the left were trees filled with yellow, pink, and red apples. The trees on the other side were bare of fruit now, their season having passed.

"I overheard a weird conversation between David and Wilfred," Kaylee said hesitantly. Did she really want to taint such a lovely experience with this conversation? But what else could she do? It was all she could think about. "I got the impression that David wants to buy Wilfred's land."

Mary stared out at the orchard. "I can see the logic of that, since it's adjacent to his. But what a shame if this all became houses. That's happened so often here on the island."

With the value of island land and the desirability of second homes, Kaylee could understand the situation—but that didn't mean she had to like it. She may be a transplant to the island rather than a lifelong resident like Mary, but she had lived there long enough to bristle at the idea of greed or commercialism overrunning the rural character that was part of Orcas Island's charm.

A farmhouse nestled among shade trees came into view at the end of the road. A couple of barns and low metal buildings dotted the surrounding landscape. Near one barn, chickens pecked at the grass. Goats and a horse grazed alongside the chickens, and they raised their heads in curiosity as Kaylee drove by.

Kaylee parked alongside several other cars resting next to the longest outbuilding, which had a sign that said *Bates Fruit Packing House* mounted on the wall. She left Bear in the car, windows open, because he wasn't allowed inside a food handling area. But on the brisk fall day, he was content with another biscuit to gnaw on and Kaylee's promise that they wouldn't be long.

Kaylee and Mary entered the building and found Jessica, DeeDee, Reese, Lorraine, and Wilfred standing behind a barrier that prevented contamination.

"Welcome to Bates's, ladies," Wilfred said kindly. "Now that you're here, I'll start the tour."

As he led the small group around from station to station, he explained several processes carried out in the building, including washing, inspection, grading, and packing fruit.

"Does all of the fruit make it into the grocery store?" Jessica asked.

"Only the top-grade fruit does," Wilfred answered. "Anything else is sold for processing into applesauce or jelly and the like."

Kaylee nodded toward a sign on the wall that said *USDA Certified Organic.* "And you're organic?"

"Yes ma'am, 100 percent," Wilfred said proudly.

Mary adjusted her glasses, studying the sign. "That's not easy to get."

"It isn't. It starts with the soil and affects every step of the process." Wilfred began listing criteria on his fingers. "No commercial fertilizers, pesticides, or herbicides allowed. And we have to get our water tested on a regular basis too."

His audience murmured in amazement and appreciation. Kaylee knew from other apple growers that it was hard producing a flawless apple without chemicals. The fruit was subject to a number of blights and insect attacks. But judging by the ones rotating on the nearby conveyor, Wilfred had the technique down.

"Get this," Lorraine said. "You can't even pack commercial

apples in the same room with organic." Her eyes were aglow with fervor. "But who would mix anyway? It's like my cleaning business. We're green, green, green. That's why we named it what we did."

"Makes sense," Jessica said. "I'll have to ask you for recommendations regarding products. I've been meaning to go more eco-friendly myself."

Before Lorraine could respond, Floyd walked into the building, glanced around, then hurried to join the others.

"Where have you been?" Lorraine asked him, but Kaylee didn't catch his mumbled response.

"Right this way to the orchard, folks," Wilfred said, waving his arm in a wide sweep toward a pair of double doors.

"I'm going to go get Bear," Kaylee told her friends. "He'd love a walk."

"We'll wait for you," DeeDee said.

Kaylee hurried toward the exit, eager not to hold everyone up. As she passed by Lorraine and her son, she heard the older woman ask, "What did David say about the lessons?"

Floyd grunted in disgust. "He said no, even though you already paid for them. He said I was the least natural pilot he'd ever had the misfortune of teaching—"

Feeling like she was eavesdropping, Kaylee tuned out their conversation and continued on to her vehicle. But she gathered that the less-than-tactful David had profoundly insulted poor Floyd.

Out in the fragrant orchard, the group—minus Floyd, who had disappeared—strolled between rows of trees. As Kaylee had predicted, Bear loved sniffing at the trees and grass, even the sweet, fallen apples lying here and there.

"We grow Honeycrisp, Gala, Braeburn, and Cripps Pink." Wilfred plucked apples and handed them out. "Just wipe them to make sure there's no dust. No chemicals on that skin. Never have been, ever since my granddad planted these trees."

Kaylee bit into hers with pleasure, enjoying the tart yet sweet taste as it hit her tongue. *Nothing like a ripe, crisp* Malus pumila *off the tree.* Referring to plants by their Latin names was a hard habit to break despite having traded the classroom for the florist studio a few years earlier. Before moving to Orcas Island to take over her grandmother's business, Kaylee had been a plant taxonomy professor at the University of Washington—and occasional forensic botany consultant for the police, which she still dabbled in as needed with the island sheriff's department.

"We'll be selling a lot of our apples at the fest," Wilfred said. "It's a banner year."

"You can say that again." Reese gestured toward the closest tree. "These branches have so many apples on them, they're practically groaning."

Dusk was falling, the first few pinpricks of stars appearing in the indigo sky. Wilfred wrapped up the tour, and the group started back toward the parking lot. Wilfred and Lorraine led the way, and DeeDee and Kaylee followed behind them with the rest of the visitors bringing up the rear.

"What on earth did David Smythe want after the meeting?" Lorraine asked Wilfred as they walked, acid lacing her tone. "And by the way, he was terribly rude to my poor Floyd. Hopefully you can give him lessons. He's dying to learn to fly."

DeeDee and Kaylee silently exchanged concerned looks as Lorraine unloaded on Wilfred.

"He told me he's going to get my land." Wilfred spread his arms out wide. "I told him it's not for sale."

While this was technically true, Kaylee reflected, it didn't convey the menacing confidence the developer had exuded during the discussion. Was Wilfred in denial about the threat to his orchard and home? But how could David Smythe force him to sell? Maybe he was only a blowhard and Wilfred knew it.

"How can you be so calm?" Lorraine demanded, her voice as tart as any Granny Smith apple.

Wilfred settled his hat more firmly on his head. "Well, after we had that knock-down-drag-out last week in the middle of the FBO, I decided I wasn't going to let him get under my skin anymore."

Lorraine huffed out air. "I don't trust that man an inch. You can ask Brett about him. I can't believe Brett is in business with him, after what David did to Brett's father. Poor Lon." She snorted. "I guess money talks. Although I've heard David isn't exactly solvent."

"I wouldn't know about that," Wilfred said. "But about Floyd, sure I'll give him a lesson or two. He can see how he likes it before he commits long-term."

DeeDee grasped Kaylee's arm and held her back. Once the others were out of earshot, she said, "We need to find Wilfred's son, Kip. I have a feeling my godfather is in over his head." Lorraine glanced over her shoulder at them, so DeeDee added, "Let's talk tomorrow, at your shop."

"Come by before you open," Kaylee offered. "We'll be there."

DeeDee nodded agreement. "See you then. I'll bring the coffee."

The next morning, the bookstore owner showed up at the front door of the grand old Victorian mansion that housed The Flower Patch. As promised, she had cups of coffee as well as a paper sack from Death by Chocolate in her hands.

"How do caramel apple muffins sound?" DeeDee asked,

setting her offerings down on the counter.

"Perfect." Kaylee handed a coffee to Mary, then took one for herself and pulled off the lid to add cream.

"Hi, guys," Jessica sang out as she popped through the door behind DeeDee. Since the bakery was next door, she hadn't bothered with a coat. Instead, she wore an apron with *Death by Chocolate* emblazoned across the bib. "I thought I'd pop over and join you. Gretchen can handle the counter."

"I'm glad you did." Kaylee opened the sack of muffins while Mary grabbed small paper plates and napkins from the back. "Are you making these to sell at the Apple Fest?"

Jessica nodded. "There aren't a lot of good recipes combining chocolate and apples, so I'm stepping outside my comfort zone and—gasp!—trying out recipes that don't include chocolate. Please don't hold back with your opinions. I can't serve bad muffins at the festival and leave our guests with a poor impression of us."

"Nothing bad has ever come from your kitchen, chocolate or not," Mary said, handing out plates.

"Said completely objectively, of course," Kaylee teased, knowing that Mary was both right about Jessica's baking skills and too kind to ever say a disparaging word against their friend.

There was a short silence while they all sampled the muffins, then Mary said, "I think you've got a winner. The taste reminds me of caramel apples, but better, since there's no sticky mess."

"Polly would argue that the sticky mess is the best part," DeeDee said.

The baker gave her a thumbs-up. "Thanks. I think the apples have a particularly good consistency. I'm planning to buy from Wilfred for all my Apple Fest recipes. He said I could pick up a few cases next time I go out."

"I enjoyed visiting the orchard last night," Kaylee said. "What a lovely place. Bear liked it too."

Bear, who was sniffing around for stray crumbs, wagged his tail at the mention of his name, then returned to his task.

DeeDee's mouth turned down. "I'm worried about Wilfred. He's under a lot of pressure."

"To sell, you mean?" Mary finished off the last piece of her muffin.

"Exactly. David Smythe is being pretty pushy about it." DeeDee set down her cup and began to pace. "The problem is, he's getting older, obviously, and there isn't anyone to take over for him. Well, except his son."

"What's the story with that?" Kaylee asked. "You said we have to find him?"

DeeDee pivoted on her boot heel and walked back the other way. "He and his father had a falling out a few years ago, and Wilfred hasn't heard from him since." She grimaced. "I don't think Kip approves of Lorraine, or her son."

"That's a bit childish, isn't it?" Mary crossed her arms. "Wilfred's wife has been gone for a decade. Surely he deserves some companionship."

"That does sound odd." Jessica drained her cup. "Kip worked for Luke in the accounting practice about five years ago. As I recall, he was a low-key person, not the type to get emotional."

DeeDee ran a hand through her hair. "That's just it—he's not. Maybe he knows something about those two we don't." She pursed her lips. "They're pretty new to the island. They've only been here about three years."

Kaylee laughed. "Is that really a strike against them?" She'd faced a little resistance from longtime residents when she'd first moved to Orcas Island. Thankfully that had all gone by the wayside and she was now an accepted member of the community.

"I only meant that we don't know their background," DeeDee said with an apologetic smile. "Kip was living in Seattle then, so maybe he did."

"He was logging hours toward a CPA license when he worked for Luke," Jessica put in. "I wonder if he ever took the test."

"How old is he?" Kaylee asked, her mind already on how they could locate the missing young man.

DeeDee returned to the counter. "In his late twenties, I think." She glanced upward, calculating. "That's right. Wilfred is sixty-three and he was thirty-five when Kip was born."

"I could see the pride that Wilfred has in the orchard," Mary said. "It would be a shame if he let it go."

DeeDee tapped one finger on the counter. "Exactly. If Wilfred wants to sell, then more power to him. But I have the feeling he's being pressured."

"I can vouch for that." Kaylee relayed the conversation she and Reese had overheard. "It sounded like David thought he had some kind of leverage."

"That does sound ominous," Mary said. "Let's look for Kip, then. We can at least apprise him of the situation. Maybe he'll know what to do."

"I can ask Luke if he stayed in touch," Jessica said. She pulled out her phone and sent a text.

"Thanks, Jess." DeeDee closed her eyes for a moment, then glanced back up at her friends. "I can't stand by and do nothing. Wilfred has been so good to me."

A minute later, Jessica's phone beeped. She shook her head. "Luke says he has no idea where Kip is but will check a database he has access to." A few moments later, the phone beeped again. "No go. Kip doesn't have a CPA license in Washington."

Mary groaned. "That would have been too easy."

"I did take a peek at social media," DeeDee said. "But there are a bunch of men with the name Kip Bates, believe it or not."

Kaylee had searched for people more than once. "I'll check

the directories at the library." She jotted down the information that Jessica and DeeDee knew about the young man. That would help narrow the search.

"Maybe Luke has a picture of Kip from when he worked in the office. I'll have him try to get you a photo," Jessica suggested.

The shop phone rang and Mary answered it. "Good morning, The Flower Patch. How may I help you?" As she listened to the answer, her gaze sharpened. Then she scribbled down an order. "We'll deliver the arrangement later this morning. Thanks, Brett."

"Brett?" Kaylee asked. "As in Brett Horne, the airport manager?"

"That's the one." Mary placed the order on the counter with satisfaction. "I think we've got a new customer."

Kaylee was pleased. With the foot traffic from the Apple Fest, their business would get lots of exposure. She studied the order, a tall vase with a selection of fall flowers. "Mary, let's do another one exactly like this for our booth. Seeing it more than once will reinforce us in people's minds."

"Great idea," Mary agreed.

"Good luck, you two. I'd better get to the shop." DeeDee moved toward the door, then paused. "Oh, by the way, band practice is at our house tonight. You're welcome to come over for a cookout, and we'll eat once our rock stars are rocked out."

After a chorus of assent and a short strategy session on who would bring what to dinner, DeeDee and Jessica left Mary and Kaylee to their work.

A couple of hours later, Kaylee loaded the shop's delivery van and, with an eager Bear in tow, left Mary to watch the shop and assemble the apple-themed wreaths they'd be selling at their Apple Fest booth.

Kaylee stopped at the hospital, a couple of inns, and a bank before heading out to the airfield. While driving along the access road, she slowed down when passing by the orchard. An *Open* flag hung by the entrance and a sandwich sign announced *Pick Your Own Apples*—a perfect leisure activity for a beautiful fall day.

A number of cars and trucks were parked at the airport, with groups of people gathered on the tarmac and around the hangars. A few more planes had arrived for the fly-in, including an Army-green bomber off by itself, battered but still a magnificent example of American ingenuity.

The FBO's back door was propped open so Kaylee pulled up in a temporary parking spot alongside the building. "Let me take this in, Bear, and then we'll go for a walk to check out the airplanes and the vendors."

Kaylee opened the van's rear door and grabbed the arrangement, which, due to its size, required both arms to carry. She headed into the main room and set the flowers on the reception desk as they'd been instructed. The bill was attached with tape so she pulled it off and placed it beside the vase.

No one appeared to be in the building, but a couple of doors to the adjacent rooms were open. She checked the first and found an empty office. The second door was only slightly ajar, but the light was on, so she knocked.

The lightweight door swung open when she knocked. David Smythe was sitting at the desk, a thermos of coffee on the blotter along with a mug.

But he was slouched back in his chair, eyes open and glassy. Some kind of froth rimmed his lips.

Even without checking his vital signs, Kaylee could tell he was dead.

3

Kaylee stepped backward with a gasp. Her mind went completely blank for an instant before dozens of thoughts tumbled through her mind. *David's dead . . . Call 911 . . . That can't be natural causes . . .*

With shaking hands, she patted her pockets for her phone. She'd left it in the van. She retreated from the office and dashed for the front desk, where a landline phone sat on the counter. She had barely picked up the receiver when Brett walked in, whistling. He was dressed in jeans with his shirtsleeves rolled up and an ID lanyard around his neck. His eyes went right to the flowers.

"You're the florist? Nice job," he said. "Even better than I imagined."

"Brett." Kaylee's voice was high-pitched and squeaky. She cleared her throat. "David is dead." She waved toward the office.

The manager's eyes widened as he took in her words. "David? Dead? What are you talking about?"

"Look in his office. I'm calling 911." Then realizing he might not know what to do, she called, "Wait! Don't go in there. I think it's a crime scene."

Brett released a squawk of disbelief but stayed where he was.

Kaylee gave the information to the dispatcher, who promised to have the sheriff and his deputies out there immediately. When she hung up, she discovered Brett hovering behind her, a hand over his mouth.

"What do you think happened?" the airport manager asked. "He was okay when I last saw him."

"When was that?" Kaylee asked.

Brett rubbed his temples and scrunched his eyes shut in thought. "Early this morning, when he first got here. Then I went out to talk to people. What's your name, by the way?"

As Kaylee was introducing herself, she heard heels tapping on the tile floor, coming nearer. Moments later, a woman dressed in black slacks and a floral blouse came around the corner from the back entrance. Sky-high sandals were strapped on her feet. Kaylee recognized her immediately as the blonde woman who had dropped David off—the one who had threatened to call her attorney.

"Hey, Brett." The woman didn't acknowledge Kaylee beyond a once-over that seemed to contain mild disgust. "David around?"

Brett glanced at Kaylee, who remained silent. This was not her story to tell. He sighed and stepped forward. "Pamela. I have something to tell you." He reached out and gripped her upper arm. "I hate to be the one to give you the news, but David is . . . gone. Dead. He passed away."

Pamela swayed on her feet, her long lashes fluttering. Then she wrenched her arm away from Brett's grasp "No! It can't be true."

"I'm sorry, ma'am, but it is," Kaylee said. "The sheriff will be here any minute."

"What happened?" Pamela demanded.

"We don't know," Brett said. "This lady, Kaylee, found him a few minutes ago."

The woman's head swiveled wildly as her gaze searched the otherwise empty room. "Where is he? I want to see him." She glimpsed the open office door and bolted toward it, her heels rapping on the floor.

"Stop her, Brett," Kaylee said. "Don't let her in there." Kaylee had left the door exactly as she'd found it to preserve the scene. If she'd known she would have people trying to get in there, she would have shut and locked it.

The airport manager managed to catch Pamela at the doorway, trapping her by wrapping both arms around her. Pamela clawed and flailed, then drove one heel into Brett's foot, causing him to yelp.

Just as Kaylee was considering joining the fight, a voice thundered, "What is going on here?"

Sheriff Eddie Maddox and Deputy Nick Durham entered the building, to Kaylee's great relief.

The wrestling adversaries somehow heard him and pulled apart, a red-faced Pamela straightening her blouse while Brett huffed and puffed, sending glares at the unruly woman.

"Let's take it from the top," Maddox said. "Kaylee, you called 911?"

Kaylee nodded. "I got here about twenty minutes ago and discovered David Smythe in that office over there. I could tell he was dead, so I didn't even go in."

"Good job," Nick said, his eyes beaming approval. Since moving to the island, Kaylee had become good friends with the charming deputy. He was an incorrigible flirt with most women, but he treated Kaylee like a favorite sister, for which she was grateful.

Nick was all business as he moved toward the office, gesturing for Brett and Pamela to step aside. Seeming to be over their animosity, they huddled together, watching as the deputy pushed the door open further and studied the room. Then he put on gloves and disposable foot covers to check the body and confirm death.

The sheriff approached Brett and Pamela, his notepad at the ready. "I'll need to question both of you. But first, I need to see some identification." His eyes flicked to Brett's lanyard. "You're the airport manager?"

"Yes." Brett motioned to Pamela. "And this is David's wife, Pamela Smythe." He spelled it as the sheriff wrote it down.

Eddie's eyes were sympathetic as he studied Pamela, who

stared at the floor, rubbing her upper arms with both hands. "Would you like a family liaison officer? I can call one."

She shook her head sharply. "No. I'll be all right."

"If you're sure." Maddox settled her in an empty office with the door partly open. Next he told Brett to secure the front door and put up a *Closed* sign. "We'll come and go through the back. Other deputies are on their way to keep people out of here."

"Understood," Brett said, as someone rattled the front door and then rapped, looking irritated. "But there are a lot of people around, as you can see. The official start of our fly-in isn't for a few days, but people are already arriving."

"I get that," Eddie said. "But there won't be any access to this building until we're done here."

Nick emerged from the office and conferred with the sheriff, then stepped aside to call in the crime scene techs and the coroner.

Kaylee stepped aside and called Mary. "I'm still at the airport," she told her assistant. "There's a . . . situation."

"Is the sheriff there?" Mary asked. Her tone indicated that, thanks to her former job as a police dispatcher and her experience working for Kaylee, who often found herself wrapped up in mysteries, she had a hunch what the "situation" entailed.

"Yes. If I don't make it back before closing, can you handle it?"

"Of course," Mary said. Her tone became one of concern. "What's going on? Are you and Bear all right?"

"We're fine." Kaylee glanced around, then lowered her voice. "I can't really talk about it right now, but I'll fill you in when I can."

"I get it," Mary said. "I won't say a word to anyone, not even about where you are." She paused. "But I will expect a call later. Or an update at our dinner."

Oh, the potluck. Depending on how long Kaylee had to stay, she might have to pick up something at the grocery store to contribute. She wouldn't have the time to cook—or the energy.

"Of course. I'll keep you posted." Kaylee tucked away her phone and got up. Poor Bear had been stuck in the van long enough, and she really should move the vehicle.

Deputy Alan Brooks was guarding the back entrance, standing with his arms folded across his broad chest. His blue eyes were stern as he addressed two visitors. "I'm sorry, ma'am, but I can't let you in."

Kaylee recognized Lorraine and her son, Floyd. By their attire and the buckets and equipment they were holding, she guessed they had come to work. A Deep Green Cleaning van stood nearby, its side doors open.

"Why not?" Lorraine asked. "We have a standing appointment every week to clean the building." The older woman tipped her head to the side and noticed Kaylee. "Can you tell us why we can't go in? I see they let *you* in."

"Yeah, her van's right here, Mom." Floyd rolled his eyes.

Bear, who had his nose poking out of the shop van's open window, yipped at the sight of his owner.

"Deputy Brooks." Kaylee knew him on a first-name basis, but when the officers were at work, she used their titles. "I'm going to move my van and take Bear for a little walk. If Deputy Durham needs me, please tell him where I went."

Alan tipped his hat in acknowledgment, exposing just a little more of his shaved head. "I'll be sure to do that."

As Kaylee walked toward her van, she felt the heat of Lorraine's gaze on her back. "She's working with your department?"

Actually, I'm here as a witness today. But Kaylee kept her lips firmly zipped as she opened the driver's side door and hopped in.

The deputy didn't answer Lorraine's question. "I suggest that you move your vehicle, ma'am. You're right in the way of official business. You have one minute."

Hearing the rumble of engines, Kaylee glanced toward the

road. The coroner's van was arriving, as was another official-looking SUV.

Lorraine released a yelp of surprise when she saw the new arrivals turn into the parking lot and the lettering on the van became visible. "The coroner? What's he doing here?" Lorraine gripped the deputy's forearm. "Is it Wilfred? Tell me it's not Wilfred."

"Ma'am." Brooks patiently removed her hand. "I don't know who you're talking about. Please move your vehicle. Now."

While Lorraine and Floyd finally complied, Kaylee did likewise. Once Kaylee and Lorraine were clear of the FBO's rear door, the coroner's van approached and backed in so that its rear door was facing the building. Giles Akin, the coroner and a local funeral home director, emerged from the van and hurried into the building, the word *Coroner* emblazoned on his windbreaker merely a flash as he disappeared.

Using a side lane, Kaylee drove to the rear of the lot and parked, well out of the way of crime scene traffic. She got out of the van, bringing Bear along with her.

Floyd pulled into the spot beside Kaylee's van, and Lorraine burst from her vehicle, clearly frantic. "Kaylee, tell me what's going on."

Kaylee straightened from clipping Bear's leash onto his collar. "It's not up to me to say, I'm afraid." She allowed Bear to drag her toward the edge of the lot. "But I do have a question. Why were you concerned about Wilfred? Isn't he at the orchard today?"

Lorraine plucked at her bottom lip. "I already checked there, and his part-time employee said he came over to the airport. I got worried when I saw the sheriff's deputy and then the coroner." She huffed. "Can you blame me?"

Floyd took his mother's arm as a plane buzzed overhead, clearly coming in to land. "There he is now. He was up giving a lesson."

"Let's go talk to him," Lorraine said. At her son's frown, she added, "We booked an hour here so we have time before the next job."

The pair hurried off toward the tarmac. Bear finally finished sniffing around, so Kaylee headed back to the FBO building, hoping the sheriff would take her statement soon so she could leave.

Inside, Kaylee returned to her earlier seat, keeping Bear on his leash. After a few excited lunges when he spotted his friends from the sheriff's department, he subsided and curled up under the bench.

The door to David's office was closed, so Kaylee couldn't see the crime scene, not that she particularly wanted to. The door to the office where Pamela was stationed was also shut, which probably meant she was still being questioned.

When that office door opened a few minutes later, the new widow was ushered out by Sheriff Maddox and Deputy Robyn Garcia. Robyn was wonderful with victims' families, and Kaylee could see that her presence comforted Pamela.

"Do you need someone to drive you home?" Deputy Garcia asked. "Is there someone you want us to call for you?"

Pamela shook her head, keeping her gaze on the floor. "No, I'll be fine." After some parting words from the sheriff, she trudged toward the back entrance, watching her steps. This time, her heels made only faint clicking sounds, the passion and energy she'd shown earlier seemingly drained away.

Kaylee was familiar with the numbness that followed news of a death. Granted, assuming David's death was considered suspicious, Pamela had to be a suspect in this case. Spouses almost automatically were, and this marriage hadn't been the happiest, judging from what Kaylee had witnessed.

The sheriff pivoted and spotted Kaylee on the bench. "I'll be with you in a few, Kaylee. I'm going to talk to Brett first."

Kaylee nodded. Needing to release some nervous energy, she got up to study the flyers and postings on a nearby bulletin board. A photograph of a white airplane for sale caught her eye.

The make and model, Beechcraft H18, sounded familiar. When she saw that the seller contact was David Smythe, she recalled someone mentioning that he owned this plane.

Then she saw the $200,000 price tag and swallowed a gulp. *Not exactly pocket change.*

So David had been trying to sell his airplane. Did he need the money or was he planning to upgrade? Kaylee read the flyer's text closely, only to become more intrigued. *Hate to let this beauty go, since it's been in the family for over fifty years, but it's time.* Long ownership usually meant there were important reasons spurring the sale.

A door opened and Brett, Sheriff Maddox, and Nick emerged. "Can I go out to the vendor area and check on things?" the manager asked. "Whatever is happening out there is my responsibility."

"That's fine," Eddie said. "But please don't say anything about the case until after the department makes a statement."

"And we'd like a list of the first arrivals," Nick added. "Whoever David might have talked to on his way in. You said he arrived early this morning?"

"Yes, around eight." Brett glanced out at the airfield, his expression worried. "Only a couple of pilots were here at that time. The rest were either home or at their lodgings."

"We'd like a list of who was on-site before he arrived," Nick said.

The door to David's office opened, and the coroner bustled out. With a nod, Giles took Eddie aside—but not far enough away from Kaylee that she couldn't overhear the conversation.

"Definitely of suspicious origin," Giles said. "From the odor, I'm guessing a pesticide of some kind."

Apparently also listening, Brett snorted loudly. "Pesticide? We don't have any of that on this property." He whirled around and pointed toward the parking lot. "But I'd check that farm next door if I were you."

4

Pesticide? That did sound nasty. Then something clicked in Kaylee's mind. "I'm sorry, but I couldn't help overhearing," she said. "Were you talking about the orchard, Brett?"

The airport manager had the grace to appear discomfited by his brash accusation. Or was it so brash? Maybe he was trying to cast suspicion on Wilfred. "Yeah. Farms use a lot of chemicals, right?"

"Most do," Kaylee conceded. "But the Bates farm is certified organic. That means no pesticides."

The thrust of Brett's jaw was stubborn. "They could have bought some."

Kaylee folded her arms across her chest. By that logic, anyone could have purchased the poison. Considering the contentious land development, spousal acrimony, and possible trouble with the airport manager—according to Lorraine—plenty of David's acquaintances could qualify as suspects.

"Right now we'll take a look around this building and others on the airport property," the sheriff said. "Unless you have any objections, Mr. Horne?"

"In that case we'll get a warrant." Nick pulled out a cell phone. "I can call the judge now."

Brett gestured broadly. "Go ahead. Whatever it takes to figure out who did this terrible thing." Forehead creased in distress, he ducked his head, blinking rapidly.

"I'll do an autopsy right away to see if we can narrow down the cause of death," Giles said as his assistants guided a gurney out of David's office.

"That would be helpful," Eddie said. "Kaylee, shall we step

into a vacant office?" He indicated the room he had just come out of with Pamela.

"Sure," Kaylee said, ready to get her interview over with so she could finally leave. Her five-minute flower delivery had turned into an hours-long ordeal.

Kaylee and Bear followed the sheriff into the office, which was actually more of a cubbyhole or former closet. A desk and a few chairs filled most of the available floor space. Flying charts covered the walls, with a pin marking the location of this particular airport. A narrow window offered a little relief from the claustrophobia the tight space could inspire.

"I'm guessing this office is only used once in a while," Eddie said, indicating the bare desk. He lowered himself into the battered desk chair.

Kaylee perched on the plastic scoop chair opposite and settled Bear on her lap. She buried her nose in his soft fur, longing to have the interview over with.

"All right, Kaylee. I won't keep you long. I know you've experienced an ordeal." Maddox's dark eyes glinted with understanding. "Take me through today, starting with why you came out here."

She told him about the bouquet order, how the building had been empty when she arrived, and then finding David. She also relayed her conversations with Lorraine and Floyd as well as the encounter with Pamela and Brett.

"I appreciate your attention to detail," Maddox said, focused on jotting down everything Kaylee said.

"Do you think the pesticide was in the coffee?" Kaylee asked. She thought so, but perhaps David had ingested the poison before coming to the airport. The toxin's effects could have been immediate or delayed, depending on what it was.

"Possibly." Maddox cocked his head. "Probably, judging by the scene. But we won't jump to any conclusions. The thermos and cup are on their way to be tested."

If the poison was in the coffee, Kaylee wondered how someone had managed to tamper with it. David and his thermos must have been separated at some point.

Apparently thinking along similar lines, Eddie said, "We're going to have to track his movements from the minute he got up. We already have a team going to his house." He named the street, located in Turtle Cove's downtown area.

When he didn't immediately ask another question, Kaylee prompted, "Is there anything else you need from me?"

He considered that for a moment. "Not right now. If you remember anything . . . well, you know the drill."

Kaylee stood, picking up Bear as she did. "David wasn't the most pleasant man, but he didn't deserve this." She reached for her tote. "I'll be around if you need me."

The first thing Kaylee did when she got into the van was call Mary. "I'm finished talking to the sheriff, so I can come back to the shop if you need me."

"Actually I'm fine," Mary said. "Why don't you go home and take a break? I'll see you at the party."

Kaylee exhaled a great gust of air. "Actually, that sounds wonderful. I'm wiped out." She propped her head up with one hand, her elbow resting on the window ledge. The afternoon was well advanced and the bright, slanting sunlight felt good on her skin.

"I'll bet you are." Mary hesitated, and Kaylee sensed her curiosity. But instead of probing, she merely said, "I'll see you tonight."

A short while later, Kaylee pulled into the driveway of Wildflower Cottage, relieved to be home. First she'd boil potatoes so she could make salad for that evening's potluck, and then she would take a long hot shower.

And try to forget stumbling across David Smythe's body.

As she climbed out of the vehicle, letting Bear trot to the door ahead of her, she wondered what made her such a magnet for murder and mystery.

Then a thought struck as she unlocked the door. She also had a good track record—so far—of solving crimes. There was a bit of satisfaction in that, but she hoped the sheriff's department would take care of this one without her help. She sighed. *If not, well, with any luck my streak will continue.*

Feeling marginally better, she fed Bear an early supper and peeled potatoes. After they were cooked, she put them in the refrigerator to cool and went to get cleaned up and changed.

A fresh pair of jeans, a favorite sweater, and suede moccasins made a comfortable but attractive outfit and had her feeling like a new woman. She mixed the potato salad, adding diced onion and celery along with a special dressing her grandmother had taught her, and put it in a large glass bowl with a fitted lid. Feeling refreshed, she was looking forward to the cookout.

DeeDee lived in a neighborhood close to Turtle Cove's downtown, in a yellow modified Cape Cod with three dormers and a wide, welcoming front porch. Kaylee parked on the street because the driveway was already full. She recognized most of the cars, but one or two were unfamiliar.

As she and Bear made their way up the paved drive, the driving sounds of rock music drifted from the garage. Kaylee smiled, feeling a thrill of adolescent glee at the idea of her friends in a legitimate garage band.

She paused to listen to the drumming. Reese was quite good, Kaylee realized. She supposed she shouldn't be surprised. The man never ceased to amaze her with his talents and interests.

Kaylee guessed everyone would be hanging out in back, so she circled the house via a paved path. A handful of people were gathered on the deck, either sitting at the long table or standing against the railings. DeeDee's daughters were playing a game on the grass, shouting and laughing.

"There you are." DeeDee straightened from her position against the railing as Kaylee and Bear came into view. She held out her hands for the bowl Kaylee was carrying. "Refrigerator?"

"Yes, it's potato salad." Kaylee's gaze went around the group, noticing that Wilfred and Lorraine were there, along with the Petal Pushers. That explained the other cars.

"Help yourself to a drink." DeeDee nodded toward a buffet table set up with pitchers of lemonade, iced tea, and water. "I'll be right back." She bustled through the sliding glass door into the kitchen.

"I heard you had quite the excitement at the airport today," Jessica said as Kaylee was filling a glass with water.

So the news was out. Kaylee was glad, since she didn't know how she would have been able to resist bringing up the topic otherwise.

"You're talking about David Smythe, I take it?" Kaylee took a seat at the table between Mary and Jessica, which placed her across from Wilfred and Lorraine. She still needed to be discreet and not reveal anything that might hurt the case.

Lorraine made a scoffing sound. "It was hours before the sheriff told us anything." Her glance at Kaylee wasn't exactly friendly. "But somehow you were in the know."

Kaylee frowned. "Not because I wanted to be. I . . . discovered him." Her belly flipped over at the memory.

Jessica inhaled sharply. "That's horrible, Kaylee. Are you all right?"

"No wonder you could barely talk on the phone," Mary said. "I could tell you were in shock." She reached over and gave Kaylee's forearm a comforting squeeze.

DeeDee must have heard all this through the open door,

because when she stepped out, she went right to Kaylee and gave her a hug. "You poor thing."

Zoe and Polly noticed their mother's action and ran onto the deck to join in. "Poor Kaylee," Polly echoed. She gave Kaylee a kiss on the cheek. "I hope that makes it all better."

Kaylee laughed. "It does. Thank you."

Lorraine's expression had remained sour. "It's a tragedy all right, but I can't help but be glad of one thing. He won't be bugging Wilfred about selling his property anymore."

Folding his arms, Wilfred sat back in his seat. "Let's not get into that now, dear."

"Why not?" Lorraine snorted derisively. "I'm only saying what everyone is thinking."

"Little pitchers have big ears," DeeDee warned, tipping her head toward her daughters. "Let's leave the topic alone for now." She strode to the grill and turned on the flame. "I will say that I hope people back off about the development now, Wilfred. I know you love that orchard."

Polly grasped Wilfred's arm. "We love it too, Uncle Wilfred. Can I come pick apples soon?" She grinned at him, revealing a missing front tooth.

Wilfred smiled at the girl. "You'd better hurry. Apples are getting so ripe, they're falling right off the tree." He made a gesture to demonstrate, ending with a loud "plop" on Polly's head.

Polly whirled to face her mother. "Did you hear that, Mom? We'd better go pick those apples before the animals get them."

Lorraine hooted. "Animals? What are you talking about?"

"Deer like apples that fall on the ground," Polly explained. "My teacher told us that."

"She's right," Wilfred said. "In fact, I leave some on the ground all winter for them to nibble on."

Zoe, who had been chatting about school with Mary,

glanced up. "Really? I hope we can visit you and see the deer."

"We'll plan on it," Wilfred promised with a grandfatherly wink.

DeeDee checked the grill and lowered the heat. "We're about ready to start cooking." She perched on a chair at the table. "Do you still need help tomorrow, Wilfred?"

He nodded. "If you have time. Like I told Polly, the apples are coming in almost too fast. I'm short pickers this year."

"I'm going to pick for an hour or two in the morning," DeeDee informed the other Petal Pushers. "Do you want to come along? I'll bring breakfast."

Mary, Jessica, and Kaylee all agreed readily.

"I wish we could go," Zoe said wistfully, a pleading expression on her face.

Her sister chimed in with a loud, "Please?"

"Me too, but you've got school." DeeDee smiled ruefully at their cries of disappointment.

The side door to the garage opened and the men emerged, laughing and joking.

"I thought it was awful quiet in there," DeeDee called.

"As long as it was awful quiet, not awful period, then we're in business," Andy Wilcox said, running a hand over his receding hairline. He and Reese wore faded classic rock band T-shirts, as did Herb, Mary's husband, who also sported a red bandanna tied around his forehead. The usually buttoned-down Luke wore a black sleeveless shirt that revealed toned arms.

"Do you guys have a name yet?" Jessica asked, her eyes sparkling up at her handsome husband.

"We sure do." Luke struck a pose, followed by the other guys. "We're the Appleseeds."

Everyone laughed.

"If only one of you was named Johnny," DeeDee joked, then pulled out her phone. "Stand by the rail. I'm going to take a publicity shot." She took several photos before grinning in satisfaction. "This one is for the poster."

That lighthearted spirit carried the night, and the cookout was a lot of fun, characterized by the laughter and good-natured teasing Kaylee enjoyed about her group of friends. For a little while, she was able to put David Smythe's death out of her mind.

But as she drove through the moonlit night toward home, her thoughts turned to the day's events. Was David's death related to the proposed fly-in community development? Had someone who opposed the project killed him? But that wasn't quite right. Since he was married, his wife would probably carry on with the project. Getting rid of David was only a temporary solution. Did that mean that Pamela was in danger?

Kaylee did wonder what the pilot had meant when he threatened Wilfred. Did he have some leverage he could use against the farmer so he was forced to sell? She couldn't imagine what it would be.

As for Pamela, she certainly hadn't appeared happy in her marriage, but perhaps it was merely a rocky patch in an otherwise happy relationship. Every couple was different, and she had certainly seemed distraught at learning of David's death.

When Kaylee pulled into her driveway, she resolved to shelve her ruminations about David Smythe so she could get a good night's sleep for the active week ahead, starting with her shift picking apples the next morning. Unsettling as David's death was, she wasn't about to let it ruin the week for everyone in Turtle Cove.

The next morning, Kaylee left Bear at Wildflower Cottage to head to the farm. She wasn't quite sure what picking would entail, so instead of risking him being stuck in her car for hours, she gave him a chew toy and a promise to return later to bring him to the shop.

A low-lying fog filled the island's valleys, so Kaylee drove carefully along the winding road out to Bates Fruit Farm, mindful of the diminished visibility. When she pulled into the property, she noticed how pretty the gnarled trees were, draped in fog. She stopped for a second and snapped a picture with her phone.

Reese's truck sat next to Mary's vehicle outside the packing house, and Kaylee was glad he'd been roped into this as well. Inside, the handyman was standing with Mary, DeeDee, and Jessica, munching on foil-wrapped egg sandwiches.

"There you are," Mary said. "We were wondering if you'd decided sleep sounded better than picking apples."

Kaylee took the sandwich DeeDee handed her and unwrapped it. "And miss DeeDee's famed egg sandwiches? No way."

"Thanks, team," Wilfred said, striding up to them. "I really appreciate your help. We've got some Honeycrisps that need to be picked. All the equipment is in the orchard already."

They followed the farmer down a gravel path about a hundred yards to a stand of trees covered with red-and-yellow apples. A trailer with empty bins was hitched to a parked all-terrain vehicle.

Wilfred handed out canvas sacks. "Sling this around your shoulders like so." He demonstrated, then walked over to the closest tree. "When you pick, lift *up* on the apple. Don't pull down. If it's ready, it will come off. Don't force them." He had each of them try picking an apple, then pronounced them ready. "When your bag is full, open the bottom and release your apples into the bins. When the bins are filled, I'll drive the ATV back to the packing shed."

Wooden ladders leaned against a couple of trees, and Reese and Jessica offered to do the upper branches while the others focused on the fruit within reach.

They were just getting started when a sheriff's cruiser came up the driveway. As soon as it was parked, Nick stepped out.

He tipped his hat at the group, keen eyes searching each face. "Wilfred Bates? I have a warrant to search your property."

5

"A warrant? For what?" DeeDee demanded. She glared at the deputy. "You've got to be kidding, Nick Durham."

Nick adjusted his stance, clearly uncomfortable. "I'm afraid not." He handed the papers to Wilfred. "This is what we're looking for, and where."

Wilfred's snowy brows rose. "Pesticide? You won't find any on this property. I don't use it. Ever. I'd lose my certification."

"So David *was* poisoned?" Kaylee asked Nick. "And you didn't find anything at the airport?"

Nick pursed his lips, avoiding Kaylee's gaze as he accepted the warrant back from Wilfred. "We're going to go search. Might take a couple of hours or so." He climbed back into the cruiser and drove off, gravel spitting from the tires.

"I'd better get up there." Wilfred stared after the vehicle, settling his hat more firmly on his head. "I can't imagine why they're searching my farm. I didn't have anything to do with David's death."

Kaylee could understand it from the sheriff's point of view, unfortunately. Wilfred had been in conflict with the dead man, and after coming up short at the airport, the sheriff's department had widened their search. Exactly as Brett had suggested, she realized with a tingle of suspicion. As for Nick's obvious discomfort with the situation, she sympathized. He had to do his job according to protocol, even if his friends didn't agree.

"What should we do?" DeeDee asked, gnawing at her lip. "This is really upsetting."

"Why don't we pick apples as planned?" Mary suggested.

"There's no point in wasting time fretting, and that way we can still be helping."

DeeDee straightened her shoulders. "You're right." She gave a half-hearted laugh. "They won't find anything, so why worry?"

With Reese's assistance, Wilfred unhitched the trailer from the ATV and zoomed off. They began to pick, each choosing a tree. Kaylee found the work soothing and meditative. She had to focus on the apples, gently testing each to discover which ones were ready. She supposed with experience she might even be able to tell on sight.

"Did you know it was poison?" DeeDee's question interrupted her aimless thoughts.

"The coroner said something about it, yes," Kaylee said with caution. "I couldn't tell you last night because it wasn't official."

Mary stopped picking. "Of course not. We get that. But now that it's out there, fill us in."

Jessica clambered down her ladder. "Yes, please do. Especially since DeeDee's godfather is now being implicated."

"How did that happen?" DeeDee scowled. "Wilfred wouldn't hurt a fly."

Kaylee sighed. "Brett suggested they check the farm out. I told the sheriff the orchard is organic, but obviously that didn't matter."

DeeDee opened her mouth in protest, but Mary beat her to it. "I know it's upsetting, DeeDee, but Kaylee couldn't warn Wilfred. She might have had an obstruction of justice charge slapped against her if she had."

"Not only that," Kaylee said, "but I didn't want to mess up the case, even by accident. I want whoever killed David to be brought to justice." At DeeDee's glower, she raised a hand. "And no, I don't believe for a minute that Wilfred had anything to do with it."

"Let's take one thing at a time," Reese chimed in. "Right now, Wilfred needs apples picked. So let's go."

They returned to picking and working together, soon filling the two big bins. But Wilfred hadn't returned with the ATV.

"What should we do now?" DeeDee asked.

"I'll go up to the house and get the ATV," Reese offered. "Then I'll take the bins to the packing house, unload them with the forklift, and get empty ones." At their agreement, he took off his canvas bag and trotted down the gravel path.

The rest of the group waited quietly. The mist was thinning now, and sunshine was beginning to filter through. The warmth felt good on Kaylee's shoulders.

"I could use another cup of coffee," Jessica said. She yawned. "Working in the fresh air is so relaxing."

Normally Kaylee would agree with Jessica's assessment, but anxiety was knotting in her belly. She wished she knew what was going on with Wilfred and the search.

Her cell phone rang in her pocket. She dug it out and answered immediately. "Reese, what's going on? Are you having trouble with the equipment?"

"Kaylee, you guys need to get up here. They're arresting Wilfred."

A chill ran through Kaylee at his words. *Wilfred?* While she trusted and respected the sheriff's department, she couldn't quite understand this decision. "We'll be right there."

"What is it, Kaylee?" DeeDee asked, her eyes wide and frightened.

Kaylee grimaced, hating to confirm her friend's fears. "They're arresting Wilfred."

"You're kidding." DeeDee's face twisted in shock. "For murder?" She whirled and dashed toward the packing house.

Jessica sprinted after her.

"Go on ahead, Kaylee," Mary said. "I'm in good shape, but I can't run that fast."

Kaylee was torn. She wanted to find out what was going on, but she hated to leave Mary behind. "Are you sure?"

"I am." Mary made a shooing motion. "Go on, scoot."

Kaylee ran after her friends, grateful they hadn't gone deep into the orchard. Panting for breath, she arrived at the packing house, where she saw DeeDee, Jessica, and Reese watching while Nick assisted Wilfred into the back of the cruiser, his wrists cuffed.

"What's going on?" Kaylee asked Reese.

"They found something inside an outbuilding," he murmured.

Kaylee's heart sank. If it matched whatever killed David, Wilfred could well be found guilty.

"This is all a mistake, Nick," DeeDee pleaded. "He's being framed." She began to cry, and Jessica wrapped her arms around her.

Nick's eyes held compassion, and by the way he studied DeeDee, Kaylee could tell he felt terrible about the situation. "I'm sorry, DeeDee. But we have to follow protocol."

Kaylee knew they must have a very good reason to arrest Wilfred. Probable cause that indicated he had committed murder as well as enough evidence for the district attorney to ask for an indictment.

Another vehicle came racing up the driveway, raising a cloud of dust. As it skidded to a stop, Kaylee saw it was the Deep Green Cleaning van. The driver's side door swung open and Lorraine jumped out. She ran to join them, white sneakers flashing.

"Wilfred!" she called. "I came as soon as I could." She whirled to face the deputy. "What is going on here?"

Nick repressed a sigh. "I'm sorry, ma'am, who are you?"

Lorraine crossed her arms, scowling. "I'm Wilfred's fiancée." At this, DeeDee opened her mouth, but Lorraine held up a hand before she could protest. "I insist on knowing why he is sitting in your cruiser."

This time Nick's sigh was a little less hidden. "I can't discuss that with you, ma'am. Now if you'll excuse me, I've got to head to the station."

Lorraine bent toward the cruiser, shouting so Wilfred could hear her through the glass. "I'll meet you at the station, dear. I'll call my attorney." After he nodded in response, she trotted toward her van and drove off.

The cruisers soon followed, leaving the farm feeling strangely forlorn. Mary appeared at the edge of the orchard, and in mutual consent, everyone remained silent until she reached the group.

"What did I miss?" Mary's eyes went to each face. "I can tell right off that it wasn't good."

Kaylee explained what had happened, to Mary's gasps of dismay.

"Surely Eddie's barking up the wrong tree with this," Mary said.

"Absolutely," Jessica agreed.

"I'm so glad you all understand that Wilfred is innocent." DeeDee dabbed at her eyes. "And another thing. I don't believe for a minute that Wilfred and Lorraine are engaged."

"What's that?" Mary cocked her head in surprise.

"Lorraine claimed they were engaged," Kaylee explained. "But I think it was so Nick would treat her like next of kin." *At least I hope that was her reason.* It would hurt DeeDee if Wilfred had hidden his engagement from her. But of course DeeDee and Wilfred had bigger problems at the moment.

DeeDee crumpled her tissue in her hand. "What should we do now?"

"Now we figure out who killed David and get your godfather off the hook," Jessica said staunchly. "Right, Kaylee?"

Kaylee felt the mantle of responsibility settle on her shoulders. The sheriff had the wrong man, and she couldn't stay out of it any longer. "We can try." She allowed herself to wallow a moment in helpless confusion, then pulled herself together with a deep breath. "Okay, what do we actually know so far?"

"That's the spirit," Mary said. "We have to begin somewhere, see where it leads us."

"When I got back here, they had just found something in that shed over there." Reese pointed to a small, ramshackle structure that appeared ready to fall over, now wrapped in crime scene tape.

"They *were* thorough, weren't they?" Kaylee studied the shed. It would have been an easy building to overlook, but perhaps that had drawn more suspicion, not less.

The group walked together over to the outbuilding. A shiny padlock secured the door and the two front windows were boarded over.

"If the poison was planted, how did someone get it in there?" Jessica asked.

"I have no idea," Reese said. "From what I heard, Wilfred had the only key on his key ring. He said he didn't like to let anyone go in there because it's not safe."

Kaylee circled the small building, which was nestled in a thicket of shrubs and brambles. The fact that Wilfred was the only one with access didn't bode well for him. Someone would have had to either copy the key or get in another way. With luck, she'd figure out what that other route might be, if there was one.

There was another window on the back of the shed, almost hidden behind a clutter of old boards and pieces of metal. Could someone have climbed in that way? Kaylee studied the brambles for signs that somebody had pushed through the thick tangle.

The others came around the corner. "What are you doing?" DeeDee asked. "It's a mess back here."

"I think someone could have gotten in that way." Kaylee pointed to the grimy window. "With the padlock on the door, they probably thought the shed was a pretty secure hiding place."

"We should check it out." Jessica eyed the brambles, then

her jeans. "But these are new."

"I'll go," Kaylee said. "I'm wearing an old pair." She began wading toward the shed, feeling the thorns tug at her jeans. In addition, pieces of wood and old shingles littered the ground, which meant she had to step with care or risk a rusty nail piercing her sneaker. When had her last tetanus shot been? She could never remember.

"Wait for me," Reese said. He followed Kaylee's path, sliding through sideways the way she had to avoid the thorns.

Kaylee reached the stacks of wood blocking access to the window. Before she had a chance to wonder how they would access the shed now, Reese had donned gloves from his back pocket and begun moving the debris so they could get close enough to touch the glass. He reached over and pushed on the window sash.

The window slid neatly upward, creating enough space for a fairly large person to crawl through. Several cinder blocks lying nearby might have provided a boost.

"It's not proof," Kaylee said, "but it certainly creates the possibility that someone climbed in there and left the poison."

"But why?" DeeDee ran her hands through her hair, making the sun-bleached locks stick out. "To frame my godfather?"

"Could be," Kaylee said. Wilfred's conflict with the deceased pilot might have made the idea attractive to the real killer. She edged back a couple of steps and took several photographs. "I'll show these to Nick and see what he thinks." She'd have to tread carefully with him, of course. The last thing she wanted was to step on the department's toes and ruin a good relationship. That definitely wouldn't help Wilfred either.

Reese closed the window, then he and Kaylee picked their way back through the brambles to rejoin the others.

"I'd better go down to the station," DeeDee said. "I want to make sure Wilfred has good representation."

"I can go open up the shop, Kaylee," Mary offered.

"Thanks," Kaylee said. "I want to run home and get Bear."

"I should get to work too." Jessica smirked. "Gretchen says she wants more responsibility, but we'll see how a busy weekday morning treated her."

As the group trudged through the field toward the farm buildings, DeeDee asked Kaylee, "Did you have a chance to look for Kip Bates yet? I think he should know about his dad's arrest, don't you?"

Kaylee's heart sank. She had been so busy she hadn't given Kip a thought. But DeeDee was right. If ever Wilfred needed his son, it was now. "I'll squeeze in a trip to the library before I pick up Bear." She glanced at Mary. "If that's okay with my right-hand woman." Kaylee tried to be mindful of not overburdening her assistant.

"The main thing on my plate is making more apple wreaths and decorations for the Apple Fest," Mary said.

"I'll certainly help you with that," Kaylee promised. "I'll stay late if I have to."

A cloud of dust from the driveway announced the arrival of another vehicle. As the group approached the packing house, a Deep Green Cleaning van pulled in and jerked to a stop, parked at such an angle they couldn't see the driver.

"Is Lorraine back already?" DeeDee asked. "That was fast."

The driver's side door opened and Floyd slid out. He adjusted his pant legs, grabbed a messenger bag and a bottle of water from inside, and began walking their way.

"Hey, how's it going?" he asked. "You guys been out picking apples?" From his calm demeanor, Kaylee guessed he hadn't heard about Wilfred's arrest.

The friends exchanged glances, not sure how to answer him.

DeeDee put up a hand, indicating that she would take the lead. "You didn't hear the news, Floyd?"

He stopped short, his shoulders sagging. "Is everyone okay? Mom? Wilfred?" Pink spots flared on his plump cheeks.

DeeDee dragged in a deep breath. "I'm not sure how to break this to you, but Wilfred was arrested this morning."

"Arrested? For what?" His voice, not deep to begin with, rose to a squeak.

"They think he killed David Smythe," DeeDee said, her own voice breaking. "They found proof."

"What proof?" Floyd's face crumpled in distress. Then he barked a laugh. "They found poison here? At an organic farm? That's ridiculous."

"Exactly," DeeDee said. "Wilfred and your mother are at the station now."

"They need me." Floyd whirled and bolted for the van. He jumped in and floored it back down the driveway.

6

A short while later, Kaylee was sitting in the library searching databases for Kip Bates when her cell phone vibrated with an incoming text from DeeDee. *Got a minute?*

Kaylee sent a quick message back that she'd call shortly, then headed for the exit. Outside, she found a sheltered spot and dialed her friend.

"Thanks so much for calling me." DeeDee took a deep, shuddering breath. "I'm just leaving the sheriff's."

"What's going on?" Kaylee couldn't imagine how DeeDee felt about seeing her beloved godfather in the grip of the law, his whole future at stake.

DeeDee lowered her voice to nearly a whisper, as if it pained her to say the words. "Apparently they found his fingerprint on David's thermos. That's their main evidence other than the poison."

A fingerprint on David's thermos? That *was* bad, although there could be many reasons that might have happened considering they both worked out of the same airport. "So what's next?"

"Wilfred's preliminary hearing is tomorrow morning. We're hoping that he'll be awarded a reasonable bail and can return home until the trial." DeeDee's voice broke on this last word. She cleared her throat and continued. "Hopefully things won't go that far, right?"

"Not if we have anything to say about it," Kaylee said, hoping to bolster her friend's spirits. "Was Floyd at the sheriff's office with you?"

"I didn't see him." DeeDee sounded puzzled. "Why?"

Kaylee thought back to how the young man had rushed

away from the farm. "I thought he would go down there since he seemed so upset about Wilfred." Not wanting to give more credence to Floyd's behavior than necessary, she changed the subject. "By the way, I'm at the library looking for Kip."

"Any luck?"

"Getting there. The library has access to some helpful databases with addresses and phone numbers." Kaylee had already narrowed her search to men of appropriate age by scanning social media.

"Thanks for doing the legwork." DeeDee was silent, and Kaylee sensed something else was coming. "How do you feel about staying at the farm with me tonight? Someone's got to take care of the animals. And keep an eye on things."

Kaylee thought over her plans for the evening, which consisted of getting into her pajamas and reading a book. "I can do that. What should we do about dinner?"

DeeDee exhaled in relief. "I'll take care of it. Thanks. I thought about inviting Andy and the girls to stay with me, but I don't want to get the girls out of their routine with school."

"I understand." Kaylee could easily imagine the early morning chaos at the Wilcox house, and how much more chaotic a sleepover at the farm could make it.

They arranged a time to meet after their shops closed, then hung up. Kaylee went back into the library to keep researching. After another half hour, she located phone numbers for three men who best fit the profile. She jotted the information in a notebook and signed off the computer, hoping that one of the men would prove to be Wilfred's son. She'd try calling them once she was outside in her car.

A few minutes later, she set her phone down in disgust. She'd managed to leave two messages, and the third number had been disconnected. "I sure hope number one or two is the right Kip," she muttered. "Otherwise it's back to searching." As she inserted the key in the ignition, her phone lit up with an incoming call. Thinking it was a Kip Bates calling back, she snatched it up and answered. "That was fast," she said. "Kaylee Bleu here."

"I didn't know you were expecting me to call," teased a familiar voice.

Kaylee nearly groaned. It was Nick Durham. "I'm sorry, I thought you were someone else. Are you calling to tell me Wilfred's arrest was a mistake?" she asked, then bit her lip, wishing she hadn't been quite so blunt.

Nick sighed. "I'll forget you said that." She heard the shuffling of papers. "I'm calling because I have a forensic botany job for you."

Her pulse quickened. Kaylee really enjoyed the cases the sheriff's department sent her way. They provided a chance to use her scientific skills while acting as an official adjunct to an investigation. It was also gratifying when her botanical knowledge helped close a case.

"Is this related to David Smythe's death?" she asked.

"Good guess. While preparing for the autopsy, the coroner discovered some plant material caught in the cuff of David's pants. We'd like you to identify it and see if it provides any clues to his movements." After a pause, he said, "I'm firmly behind the decisions this department has made. But I also want to be sure we get the full picture. Do you understand what I'm saying?"

"Loud and clear." Kaylee thought for a moment. "I'll come by the station right now."

"Great," Nick said. "See you in a few."

Kaylee called Mary to give her an update, then headed for the sheriff's department, which was located only a short distance from the library.

"Kaylee, how are you?" Aida Friedman, the department receptionist, greeted her with a big smile. She was rolling back and forth behind the long desk in her chair, placing files in various in- and out-boxes. Then she adjusted her glasses, flicked her shoulder-length blonde hair back, and popped a few Tic Tacs into her mouth.

"I'm great, thanks. How's the roller derby going?" Kaylee smiled, guessing by her energy that Aida was fully fueled with caffeine today, as usual. This energy extended to the roller rink, where the receptionist used the name Miss Demeanor while competing.

Aida pursed her lips. "Not too bad. Though we've been against some tough teams lately. You'll have to come cheer us on." She tapped out a short rhythm on the desktop. "Now what can I do for you?"

"I'm here to see Nick. He wants my input on something."

"I think I heard about that." Aida picked up her phone and announced Kaylee's arrival. "He'll be right out," she said as she hung up.

While the receptionist went back to her work, Kaylee paced the waiting area, gravitating as she often did to the most-wanted posters. What would she do if she ever saw one of these hardened criminals? Hopefully Orcas Island was too remote for any of them to find their way to the town she had grown to love.

"Kaylee?"

She whirled around as Nick's voice startled her out of her musings. "Hi," she said.

He gestured for her to follow him. "Come on back."

With another smile for Aida, Kaylee went with Nick into the back offices.

Nick led her to one of the interview rooms. "My desk is too messy for this," he explained. "Have a seat." He sat across from her and opened a manila envelope that rested on the table.

Inside was a plastic envelope containing ribbed tubular seeds with feathery tufts at the ends. "We'd like you to identify these, and also check their range." He held the small bag up to the light with a frown. "I've never seen seeds like this before."

Kaylee had an inkling what they were, but she'd need to check more closely. "They do appear unusual. With any luck, we can narrow down the locations where David might have picked them up."

Nick tucked the seed package back into the envelope and closed it. "Thank you very much." He slid the envelope across the table. "When do you think you'll be able to get to it?"

Kaylee considered his request. "Is tomorrow morning soon enough? I'm staying at Wilfred's farm tonight with DeeDee to watch the place." She wanted to do this job at Akin Funeral Chapel in Turtle Cove in case she had any questions for Giles. She could go by before opening The Flower Patch for the day. "I really need to spend the rest of this afternoon in the shop. Mary's been bearing the brunt of preparing us for the Apple Fest, and I need to help her before she gets fed up with me."

"Tomorrow is fine." Nick pushed back his chair, ready to stand. "Give me a call as soon as you know what it is and where it grows."

"I'll do that, along with anything else I come across." *The shed.* Kaylee put up a hand to stop Nick. "Hold on a second. There is something else."

He settled back into his chair. "What is it?"

Kaylee dug out her phone and scrolled through the photographs. She showed him the photo of the shed's open window, Reese standing beside it.

Nick peered at the photo. "What am I looking at?"

"That's the building where you found the poison." Kaylee pointed at the window. "I saw the door was locked and wondered if someone could have gotten in another way."

"So you tried the windows." Nick's tone was flat. Kaylee

couldn't tell if he was annoyed that she'd done it or that the team had missed it.

"Just that one. The others were boarded up. Reese used gloves and only pushed on the glass," Kaylee said. "So any prints on the frame should still be there." At the deputy's continued silence, she added, "It's a possibility that someone climbed in, right?"

Nick grunted. "I'll have someone go over and dust." He handed Kaylee the phone. "Next time call me first, okay?"

Feeling a tiny bit guilty, Kaylee agreed with a nod. "I'd better get back to the shop." She tucked her phone into her bag and grabbed the evidence envelope. "I'll let you know about the seeds."

After a brief stop at Wildflower Cottage to retrieve her eager four-legged assistant, Kaylee headed to The Flower Patch. She secured the evidence in a locked cabinet, then helped Mary fill the day's remaining orders. After those were done, they put together apple wreaths while listening to classical music and sipping decaf hazelnut coffee. Bear kept an eye on their progress from the comfort of his dog bed.

"Maybe we should hide these when we're done," Mary said, holding up a completed wreath featuring autumn leaves and faux fruit. "Last time I made some, I sold them immediately to customers here in the shop."

Kaylee smiled at a mental picture of people snatching the wreaths straight from Mary's hands. She picked up a spray of silk apple blossoms and attached it to a twisted grapevine base. "Maybe that's a good sign that they'll sell at the Apple Fest." She stood back and studied her work. "I have to admit these turned out better than I even expected." She glanced toward the front of the shop. "Let's hang one on the front door."

"Good idea. We can take orders if anyone is interested, but for *after* the fest." Mary put a proprietary hand on the completed wreaths. "These are off-limits."

After closing up the shop, Kaylee made a brief detour to the cottage to pack an overnight bag for herself and Bear, then she and her pet made the now-familiar ride out to the fruit farm. The sky was a perfect blue, and the aromas of sun-warmed grass and ripening apples drifted through her open car window.

Overhead, a few airplanes buzzed, followed by the distinctive whir of a helicopter. "It's a beautiful day for flying," Kaylee said to Bear, who had his nose poking out of the back window. She wondered if Reese would be able to continue his lessons with Wilfred. Hopefully the hearing in the morning would go well and Wilfred would be able to return to the farm.

DeeDee came out on the porch to greet them when Kaylee parked in front of the farmhouse. "Thanks again for coming," she called as she trotted down the steps. "Let's get your things inside and then we'll take care of the livestock."

After she helped gather Kaylee's bags, the trio trudged across the porch and entered the house. The front door opened into a narrow entrance hall dominated by a straight staircase on the right. As she followed DeeDee up the steps, Kaylee glimpsed a living room, dining room, and den through doors opening off of the foyer. Upstairs, there were four bedrooms, and DeeDee led her into one overlooking the orchard.

"This is nice." Kaylee put her duffel down beside the walnut four-poster bed and glanced around the small but comfortable room. The walls were pale yellow, the curtains white cotton trimmed with ball fringe. A small bathroom was attached.

"There are towels in here." DeeDee gestured toward a bureau drawer, then she opened the wardrobe door. "And you can hang things in here if you need to." The wardrobe held only a selection of coat hangers. Bear jumped up inside it and sat, making them smile.

"Come on, Bear," Kaylee said. "Time to feed the chickens."

At the mention of other animals, he jumped down and scurried toward the bedroom door.

"He does know they might peck, right?" DeeDee asked, leading the way downstairs.

"Don't worry. He's an old pro." After a few near misses with various animals and birds through the years, Bear knew when to keep his distance. But he loved to try to make friends with all creatures, even if they didn't return the favor.

DeeDee took Kaylee through the spacious, old-fashioned kitchen, where spaghetti sauce simmered on the gas range, and into a back hall. There they put barn coats on over their clothing, exchanged sneakers for rubber boots, and donned gloves.

"I feel like a real farmhand now," Kaylee quipped.

"Wait until you're done with the chores." DeeDee's tone was wry. "Then you'll qualify." As they went out the back door and crossed the yard toward the barn, DeeDee told Kaylee stories of staying at the farm as a youngster. This background helped Kaylee see why DeeDee was such a fierce defender of her beloved godfather.

"I really loved it out here," DeeDee said. "Wilfred and his late wife, Doris, were wonderful to me. Someday I'd love to own a hobby farm. I just need to convince Andy that it would be a good move."

Kaylee studied the barns and orchards and animals. Yes, it would be a lot of work, but she could see the appeal. "He runs an organic grocery store already—surely farming wouldn't be too much of a stretch. And you could cut out the middleman and raise your own goats." DeeDee made goat milk soap, which she sold at Kaylee's shop.

"Straight from the barn to the soap," DeeDee said with a chuckle. "And then to The Flower Patch."

"I bet your girls would love living on a farm."

DeeDee pushed the sliding barn door open. "They would, until it came time to clean out the stalls." She stepped into the dim space. "Grain and hay are in here."

Kaylee called to Bear, wanting to keep him in sight. He had been running around the yard, pausing to sniff all the intriguing odors. To her amusement, she saw he was engaged in a staring contest with the goats, safely enclosed in a pen. One of the goats bleated, and the dog leaped backward with a startled yip.

Kaylee laughed. "Come on, boy. Leave the goats alone." With a last glance back at his intimidating new acquaintances, Bear followed her into the barn.

DeeDee pulled a hay bale off a stack, hooking gloved fingers through the twine. "The horse and goats get hay." She hefted the bale out to the corral and Kaylee did the same with one for the goats. They broke the bales apart and spread the hay in a trough for the animals to nibble on. Then they gave them buckets of grain and filled the chicken's dishes with corn. All the animals got fresh water.

DeeDee checked the nests and found a few eggs, which they tucked into their jacket pockets. "Don't forget they're in there," she warned.

After one last check around, the women went back to the house, where they shed the work wear and stowed the eggs in the refrigerator.

"Perfect for breakfast," DeeDee said. She grabbed a pitcher from the top shelf. "Iced tea?"

"Yes, please." Kaylee stretched, pleasantly tired after her busy day. "What can I do to help?"

DeeDee poured two tall glasses and set one in front of Kaylee.

"You can sit there and drink that. I've got it all under control."

While she continued dinner preparations, Kaylee told her about the forensics assignment Nick had given her.

"You think the seeds have something to do with the case?" DeeDee slid dry spaghetti into a pot of boiling water.

"It's hard to say. From a glance I think they're from a pretty unusual plant. So the question is, where did David pick them up?" Kaylee's brow furrowed as a thought occurred to her. Didn't pilots keep logbooks that recorded destinations and dates? They'd need to cross-reference David's with whatever she determined.

DeeDee turned down the burner under the sauce. "I'll keep hoping that wherever he went is related to his death. We need another theory that doesn't involve him wanting Wilfred's land."

"I admit I didn't know David, but I did notice that he had contentious relationships with more than one person." Kaylee told DeeDee about the argument she'd witnessed between David and his wife. "And you overheard Lorraine saying that Brett had some kind of gripe. So there are avenues to explore."

DeeDee opened the oven door and popped a foil-wrapped loaf inside. "If we can get the sheriff to consider them." Her tone was glum. Then she straightened her shoulders and started foraging in the refrigerator. "But giving into doom and gloom won't help. So let's keep trying."

"I plan to," Kaylee said. "I believe Wilfred is innocent, so that means a killer is still out there." She took salad ingredients from DeeDee. "You have to let me do something."

After a delicious dinner of spaghetti, salad, and garlic bread, they spent a quiet evening reading and watching television. Then, after securing the chickens in their coop and checking on the other animals one last time, they retired upstairs. DeeDee was in the room next to Kaylee, on the other side of the shared bathroom.

Kaylee opened a window to let in some fresh evening air

before climbing into bed. Bear curled up beside her on the thick duvet and was soon snoozing, exhausted by his exciting day.

Slumber came more slowly for Kaylee, as usual in a strange place. Her thoughts kept circling around David's death, but she found more questions than answers. That always happened early in an investigation, she reminded herself. At some point, she'd be able to see how all the pieces had come together. Right now, she needed to accept that she was dealing with the murky unknown.

She had finally drifted off to sleep when Bear's barking woke her. "Bear, what are you doing?"

Outlined by moonlight, the dachshund was standing with his paws on the windowsill, barking at something outside.

"Come on, boy. You're going to wake up DeeDee. It's probably critters prowling around."

But what if a fox was trying to get into the chicken coop? Kaylee got out of bed to peer through the window.

A light was on in the barn.

7

DeeDee switched on the bathroom light and came through from her room. "What's going on? I heard Bear."

"You didn't leave a light on in the barn, did you?" Kaylee motioned for DeeDee to join her at the window. Bear, now that he had woken them, had stopped barking. He stood panting by the bedroom door, eager to chase off the intruder.

"I don't think so." DeeDee moved to the window and peered outside. "That's Wilfred's office. I peeked in there but didn't go all the way in. The light shouldn't be on."

Kaylee saw a shadow move across the lighted rectangle. "Someone's still out there. I'm calling the sheriff." She searched for her cell phone and found it under the book she'd been reading before bed. "There's no reason for somebody to be out there this time of night." She glanced at the time. "Two a.m. Yeah, something's wrong." She dialed 911 and told the dispatcher that there was a prowler at Bates Fruit Farm.

"They're sending someone right over," she told DeeDee.

"What should we do?" her friend asked, playing with the curtain. "I feel so helpless just standing here and watching. Plus I'm dying to find out who it is."

"Me too." Kaylee sympathized with DeeDee's desire for action—and information. "But it's not safe to go out there and confront an intruder."

DeeDee sucked in a breath. "Do you think it's the killer?" She kneeled on the floor and raised the screen, then poked her head outside. "I wish I could get a clear look."

As if in response to her words, the light in the barn switched off. Kaylee joined DeeDee on the floor, staring so hard at the dark building that she barely blinked. For a long moment, nothing. Then a shadow detached itself from the side of the barn and moved toward the yard.

"There he is!" DeeDee cried.

The figure paused as if he or she had heard DeeDee, then darted away into the night. A moment later, the sound of an engine starting up disrupted the quiet night.

"Hopefully the deputies will see the vehicle," Kaylee said. "Let's go check the office."

The women threw on shoes and extra layers and tiptoed downstairs. DeeDee grabbed a flashlight before she, Kaylee, and Bear headed outside. They picked their way across the dew-dampened grass. Overhead, stars freckled an inky sky, and Kaylee spotted the telltale blinking of airplane lights high above.

The animals rustled around in their stalls as they approached, and one of the goats bleated. Bear hesitated in his tracks, one front paw lifted, a pose that released some of the tension in the women.

"I wonder if the goats bleated when the intruder broke in," DeeDee said.

Kaylee wondered the same thing. "If so, I didn't hear it. But maybe that's what woke Bear."

"Something had to." DeeDee smiled down at the little dog. "You're a good watchdog, Bear. We're proud of you."

He wagged his tail in response, his whole hind end moving.

DeeDee used her sleeve to open the barn door in a different spot than usual. "In case there are prints."

The dim, dusty barn appeared unchanged, dark shapes of tools and equipment against the walls, warm odors of animals and hay drifting from the stalls. DeeDee used her flashlight beam to guide them across the floor. "I want to disturb the animals as little as possible," she explained.

The door to the office was partly open so DeeDee stood in the doorway and shined the flashlight inside—and both women gasped.

The office had been ransacked.

Papers and files were strewn across the desk, the chairs, and the floor. Books and ledgers had been dumped on top of them, the pages flapping open.

"What on earth?" DeeDee recoiled in shock.

Kaylee's chest knotted in dismay. "They were obviously searching for something." Was it related to the murder or another matter entirely? Perhaps someone was taking advantage of Wilfred being in jail. Maybe they didn't even realize that guests were staying in the house and thought they had free rein.

Had the prowler made the mess as a childish response to not finding what they sought? Or was it a smoke screen to hide true intent?

Gravel crunched and headlights swung across the yard. "The deputies must be here," Kaylee said, hoping she was right. "Let me go check."

She trotted through the dark barn, using her memory and the glow of DeeDee's light behind her to guide her way. Stopping in the open doorway, she studied the newly arrived vehicle, sagging in relief when the dome light came on and revealed two deputies.

"It's okay," she called to DeeDee. "It's the deputies." She stepped out into the yard. "Thanks for coming."

One of the deputies switched on his flashlight, careful not to shine it in her face. "Good evening, Kaylee." She recognized Deputy Tom McGregor's slight cowboy drawl, a relic from when he'd lived in Arizona. "Did you call in a report of an intruder?"

"I sure did." Kaylee pointed to Bear, who was running to greet the deputies. "Bear woke me up barking and we saw a light on in the barn." She recognized Deputy Alan Brooks as well and nodded at him in greeting.

DeeDee joined them. "Someone rifled through Wilfred's office and made a huge mess." She waved the flashlight. "Come see."

The deputies followed DeeDee to the office, with Kaylee and Bear lagging behind. Alan whistled when he saw the mess. "When did you last come in here?"

"I opened the door and peeked in earlier this evening when we came out here to feed the animals. Wilfred keeps everything in tip-top order."

"Did he keep money out here, do you know?" Tom asked.

DeeDee shrugged. "I don't think so, but you could ask him." Her smile was sad. "He's staying at the jail tonight."

Alan pressed his lips together. "I suppose there's no way to figure out what's missing."

"I'm afraid not," DeeDee said. "My godfather will have to do that, once he's free on bail." Her voice held a tiny bit of challenge.

The deputies didn't respond to DeeDee's needling, but Kaylee didn't expect them to. They must be used to dealing with resentment and anger from the families of those they arrested.

"Let's dust," Tom said. "Can we turn on some lights, Mrs. Wilcox?"

DeeDee sighed. "I was hoping to avoid that for the animals' sakes. But this is more important."

After DeeDee flipped a switch for the overhead lights, the deputies dusted for prints on the door, window, and desk area, accompanied by a chorus of noises from the goats and chickens. DeeDee threw them some extra food as a bit of a peace offering.

"Did you get anything?" Kaylee asked Alan once he was loading the equipment back in the cruiser.

He shook his head. "Too much, really. Tons of fingerprints everywhere. But we'll do our best to isolate any of interest."

She remembered the shed where the poison was found. "Did Nick tell you someone might have broken into that old shed?"

She pointed to where it sat, forlorn and empty in the dark. "The back window is unlocked."

The deputies exchanged glances. "You know, I think that's on the to-do list for the crime scene team," Tom said. "Want to go dust while we're out here?"

"I'm sure the sheriff will appreciate our initiative," Alan said. "Let's go."

"We've got a battery-operated lantern you can use." DeeDee took the lantern down from the nail where it was hanging. "You'll need it since there isn't any power out there."

The women waited until the deputies left before heading back into the house. There was a faint glow in the eastern sky. "Should we just stay up?" DeeDee asked. "The bail hearing is at nine."

Kaylee yawned, exhaustion sweeping over her. "I think I could snooze for a couple more hours. Otherwise I'll be useless tomorrow. Or today. Whatever."

DeeDee held the back door open for Kaylee. "I don't think I can. I'm so keyed up about what's going to happen." She shut the door. "Maybe I'll put on a pot of coffee and read something mindless. Try to relax at least."

"I'll stay up with you, then." When it came to a choice between sleep and helping a friend, the friend won out. Then a traitorous yawn burst from Kaylee's mouth, so wide and loud even Bear took notice.

DeeDee laughed and gave Kaylee a one-armed hug. "No, go grab some shut-eye. I'll get you up at seven, okay? We can take care of the animals and eat breakfast before heading to the courthouse."

Kaylee obediently trudged upstairs and collapsed into a deep, dreamless sleep, Bear curled up at her side. The aroma of fresh coffee woke her, and she opened her eyes to see her friend standing in the doorway, holding a mug.

"Knock, knock." DeeDee crossed the room and set the coffee

on the bedside table. She opened the curtains Kaylee had pulled, letting sunshine stream into the room.

"It looks like a beautiful day." Kaylee pushed herself to a sitting position and picked up the mug. "Thanks for bringing me coffee." She took a sip, savoring the warm brew. The first cup of coffee in the morning was always the best.

DeeDee was staring out the window, her pretty features creased with worry. But she merely said, "I'll see you downstairs in a few, okay?" She left the room, her footsteps tapping down the stairs a few seconds later.

"I really hope things go well for Wilfred today," Kaylee told Bear, stroking his silky head. "Our poor friend can't take much more."

He gazed up at her with big, sympathetic eyes that clearly conveyed he agreed.

The courthouse was a nondescript, modern brick building located on the fringe of Eastsound. Kaylee pulled into a visitor's space, noting that many spots were already full. Considering how on edge DeeDee had been feeling, Kaylee had offered to drive them to the hearing.

"Traffic court," DeeDee explained tightly. "We don't have that many bail hearings on Orcas." She released a nervous laugh that was, to Kaylee's ear, not far from a sob.

Understanding her friend's emotional turmoil, Kaylee squeezed DeeDee's hand. "Everything will be all right. Have faith in the truth."

DeeDee shifted her bleak eyes toward Kaylee. "You think we can?"

"Absolutely." Kaylee forced confidence into her voice. "Wilfred is innocent, and we're going to focus on that fact."

The two women slid out of the SUV, and Kaylee locked it. Bear had been dropped off at Mary's house, and he would go down to the shop with her.

The hearing was in Courtroom Two, according to the security guard at the front door. They were scanned by a metal detector and then allowed to enter the main building. Courtroom Two was to the right, reached through double doors that swished open and closed with barely a sound. The courtroom was thickly carpeted, with low, sound-absorbent ceiling tiles and wood furniture upholstered in blue.

Only a few people were in the room waiting for the hearing to begin, including Lorraine, who was sitting in the front row. Kaylee recognized one young man with dismay—Jocko McGee, freelance reporter. Of course the press was covering the hearing, and of course Jocko wanted a juicy story like this. No doubt Wilfred's long history and standing in the community made people even more interested in the outcome. Kaylee nudged DeeDee and indicated Jocko with her chin. DeeDee made a face.

Tyler Stevens, a local defense attorney, entered the courtroom and settled at the defendant's table. Kaylee was glad to see him. He was good at his job. Another lawyer, working for the district attorney, sat at the plaintiff's table.

A bailiff accompanied Wilfred, dressed in an orange jumpsuit, into the courtroom through a side door. DeeDee gasped and half-rose out of her seat, drawing the older man's eyes their way. He gave her a nod and a tiny smile. The bailiff settled Wilfred next to Tyler, who shook his client's hand.

Another bailiff announced, "All rise." Everyone stood up in respect as Judge Nestor Obi took his seat behind the bench.

After Judge Obi declared court in session, the charge of first-degree murder was brought forward. That meant the prosecutor believed that David's death was premeditated and deliberate, not an accident or impulsive crime. When Kaylee considered the planning that had gone into tainting David's coffee, she had to agree. That didn't mean Wilfred had done it, of course. But someone had—someone who had hated David Smythe.

Lorraine jumped to her feet. "First-degree murder? That's ridiculous! What's wrong with you?"

The judge banged his gavel. Once Lorraine stopped sputtering, Judge Obi said, "You're not helping the defendant by insulting the judge. One more outburst and I'll rule you in contempt. Is that clear?"

A chastened Lorraine nodded, then sat down. By the tense posture of her narrow shoulders as the hearing went on, Kaylee could tell she was struggling against another outburst.

"How do you plead?" the judge asked Wilfred.

"Not guilty, Your Honor." Wilfred slid a glance at Lorraine as he resumed his seat. She blew him a kiss and gave him a tiny wave.

With Wilfred's plea of innocence, the hearing moved on to bail. Tyler made an eloquent appeal for a reasonable bail, mentioning Wilfred's long history in the area, his business relationships, and his good standing in the community.

"That's certainly true," DeeDee whispered. Kaylee saw that her friend's fingers were crossed and laid her hand on DeeDee's arm.

"I'll set bail," Judge Obi said, "but Mr. Bates will need to surrender his pilot's license."

Wilfred and Tyler conferred, Wilfred obviously upset by this ruling. Tyler stood. "Your Honor, we respectfully ask you to revise your decision. Mr. Bates earns a living giving lessons to student pilots. Being unable to practice his trade would irrevocably harm his financial situation."

So would going to jail for murder. Kaylee clenched her fists, her nails biting into her palms. They had to clear Wilfred's name and find the killer.

The judge considered for a long moment then said, "You may keep your license, Mr. Bates, but you need to have someone else in the airplane with you at all times. Take any flights by yourself and bail will be revoked."

Tyler looked at his client, who nodded. "Mr. Bates can abide by that restriction, Your Honor. Thank you."

When the hearing adjourned, DeeDee caught Kaylee's arm. "Can you drive me back to the farm so I can get my car? Then I'll come back here and pick up Wilfred. He should be done with his paperwork and changing his clothes by then."

"Of course." Kaylee's brow furrowed. "Lorraine isn't going to take him home?" She glanced around and noticed the older woman was gone. She must have slipped out as soon as the hearing ended. "I guess not, since she left."

They were walking toward the exit when Jocko McGee stepped into their path. "Is it true, Mrs. Wilcox, that you're related to Wilfred Bates?"

DeeDee rolled her eyes. "No, he's my godfather. Please let us pass."

Jocko continued to block them, moving slightly aside to let other people leave. "What are your thoughts about the first-degree murder charge?"

DeeDee made an exasperated sound. "What do you think they are? He's innocent of course. And we're—"

Kaylee put a hand on DeeDee's forearm, warning her to be careful. Sometimes it was tempting to speak your mind to the press, but it wasn't always a good idea. Thankfully DeeDee bit off her words and didn't continue.

Jocko's eyes gleamed and he leaned closer. "We're what, Mrs. Wilcox? Do you have information my readers would like to know?"

"That's enough, Jocko. Mrs. Wilcox has no comment," Kaylee said sharply. "Please move. We have business to take care of."

The reporter aimed his zealous gaze at Kaylee. "What are you, her spokesperson? Shall I refer all questions to you, Kaylee?"

Kaylee sighed. "No, of course not. But I'll thank you not to bully my friend. This whole thing has been an ordeal and now we really need to go." Looping her arm through DeeDee's, she pressed past the reporter and pushed open the courtroom's swinging door.

"Can I quote you on that?" Jocko called after them.

"Don't you dare," Kaylee replied over her shoulder as they left. The stocky young man wore a broad grin. She knew Jocko didn't mean any real harm. He was just excited to write about a major case, and he could be found in the middle of anything that might give him his big break. But he had a bad habit of getting too nosy during ongoing investigations, and she'd had to fend him off before.

"Thanks, Kaylee," DeeDee said when they reached the relative safety of the nearly empty sidewalk. "I almost told him we were trying to clear Wilfred."

Kaylee pulled out her keys and pushed the unlock button. "That's where I thought you were headed. Reporters are often easy to talk to, and we can forget that they've got a job to do."

"I'll keep that in mind," DeeDee said. She mimed a zipping motion across her mouth. "If I see Jocko again, I'll run the other way."

"Today he basically trapped us, which wasn't fair." She had the feeling that Jocko would continue to snoop around. That's what she would do if she was on the trail of a hot story.

To be fair, she was doing something similar, but her motive was to solve the case, not sell papers. After taking DeeDee to the farm, she would visit Akin Funeral Chapel to examine the seeds from the victim's clothing. She'd do whatever it took to relieve the tension still troubling her friend.

The funeral home was a small, chapel-shaped stone building on Sea Cliff Avenue. As Kaylee found a parking spot at the rear of the lot, she reflected how unusual this arrangement was. In Seattle, she'd had access to state-of-the-art microscopes through the university. Here she did her forensics work wherever she had access to any microscope, including in the back room of a mortuary. The good news was she didn't have to travel to Seattle. *Whatever works, right?* As Kaylee unlocked her glove compartment and removed the evidence envelope, she felt gratitude that she could continue to use her skills.

Giles Akin greeted her when she entered. In contrast to the official coroner windbreaker he had on at the crime scene, today he wore a dark gray suit, a blue tie, and a gleaming white shirt. "How are you, Kaylee?"

"Fine, thanks." She held up the envelope. "Mind if I use the lab?"

"Nick mentioned you'd be by." Giles pushed a hand through his thick hair. "Another one for the books, eh?"

Kaylee glanced around. No one else seemed to be in the building, which held its customary flower-scented hush. "Did they determine the exact poison yet?"

Giles lowered his voice. "Zinc phosphide. It's a rodent poison, quite common."

And not something Wilfred would use on his organic farm. "I suppose it's the kind of thing you can buy anywhere?" she asked.

"Exactly. It's not expensive, either. If access was restricted, it would be easier to prove who purchased it."

Using something easily available certainly made it difficult to trace the origin and purchaser. Almost impossible, in fact. The sheriff's department would have to work backward, finding a suspect and then determining if they had access to the poison.

Kaylee sighed. "I guess I'd better get to work. Hopefully these plant materials will help." *And won't further incriminate Wilfred.*

"I thought the seeds were quite unusual." Giles accompanied Kaylee to the back room. "They were tucked right inside his pants cuff. A lot of plants do that, don't they? Hitch a ride."

"That's true," Kaylee said. One of the most fascinating elements of botany was how seeds dispersed, often using animals, birds, and even humans to find new and fertile ground. Now she needed to figure out where David had brushed against the plants.

Inside the lab, Kaylee took a moment to look up zinc phosphide on her phone. It wasn't always fatal, which led her to believe the dose must have been very high. It could also take an hour or more for symptoms to occur. When had the poison been added to David's coffee? She had found him in the late morning, well after people usually drank their first cup. The exact chain of events might be difficult if not impossible to determine. By arresting Wilfred, the sheriff's department seemed to believe it happened between David's arrival at the airport in the early morning and when she found him.

But the contamination could have happened earlier, before he arrived at the airport. In order to figure that out, she needed to know all his movements that day.

Shaking her head at this dead end, she set aside her phone and turned on the equipment. After putting together a couple of slides of the seedpods, she placed them under the viewer. As usual, she went through a methodical process to narrow down the species. Finally, after consulting a professional database, she determined the plant's name—*Microseris borealis*. Part of the aster family, it was often called northern silverpuff due to the fluffy nature of the seeds.

It was also extremely rare.

8

Kaylee took a deep breath. *So far, so good.* David had picked up seeds from a plant that grew only in select places.

Now she needed to learn exactly where.

She checked an online database for the plant's known locations. None grew on Orcas Island, so he hadn't picked up the seeds locally. She found several smaller islands listed and made a note of those. Perhaps Nick could find out if David had traveled to one of them—and why.

Using tweezers, Kaylee put the specimens back into the envelope and sealed it, along with a copy of her notes. She'd drop the evidence at the station and then go to the shop before Mary and Bear disowned her.

In the foyer, Pamela Smythe, wearing the garish lime-green windbreaker again, was speaking to Giles. Kaylee noticed the jacket had a blue-and-white flying association patch on the chest.

"I'm still in shock," Pamela said, her lips trembling. "All David and I did lately was fight, but I never expected to become a widow."

"Shock is perfectly natural considering what you've been through," Giles said, placing a comforting hand on Pamela's shoulder.

Hoping to remain unobtrusive at such a private moment, Kaylee nodded to the pair, planning to slip past and not interrupt their discussion. But Pamela put out a hand to stop her. "Kaylee, isn't it? What brings you here?" Her alarmed expression conveyed horror. "You didn't lose someone too, did you?"

"I'm here on other business," Kaylee said, feeling awkward. She could hardly share that she was digging into clues about

David's murder. "I'm sorry for your loss."

A telephone rang shrilly from behind an open door down the hall. Giles peered around but when it didn't stop, he said, "I'll need to get that. I'm not sure where Thelma went." His wife, Thelma, usually worked in the office. "Please excuse me for a minute." He hurried down the hall.

"Well, I'd better be going." Kaylee continued toward the exit, eager to leave.

But Pamela wasn't finished with her. She clutched Kaylee's jacket sleeve. "One thing that surprises me is how alone I feel." She blinked rapidly. "Everyone is so concerned and helpful but still . . ." More blinking. "Sometimes a girl could use a friend."

And I'm it? Kaylee gritted her teeth. How could she walk away now?

"Let's sit." Pamela led Kaylee to visitor seats placed along the wall. She settled herself in a chair, then clasped her hands and cocked her head, her eyes fixed on Kaylee's face. "David and I were on the fast track to divorce."

"I'm sorry to hear that." Uncomfortable with this unsought discussion of marital problems, Kaylee wasn't sure what else to say. "I had no idea."

"Really?" Pamela frowned. "Didn't you overhear our argument at the airport the other evening, before the vendor meeting? I thought I saw you in the parking lot."

"Um, I'm not sure," Kaylee fibbed. "I wasn't really paying attention." She had no idea why Pamela was discussing such personal issues with someone she barely knew. However, she realized, if she wanted to help Wilfred, she ought to hear Pamela out. After all, Pamela should be the primary suspect, not Wilfred, according to conventional law enforcement wisdom. Quite often the spouse or romantic partner was the primary suspect.

"Well, anyway," Pamela continued, "after that night, I decided

I'd had enough. So I packed up and moved out. I've been staying at the Tortoiseshell Hotel." She sniffed. "I suppose I can move back in now."

"So you didn't see David the morning he died?" Somewhat mortified she'd blurted that out so bluntly, Kaylee's skin prickled with heat while she waited for the woman's response.

Pamela's expression was shrewd. "I just told you I wasn't staying there. Why would you think—" Her phone trilled in her handbag so she broke off to pull it out.

She hadn't answered the question, Kaylee noted. Planning to dig a little more now that the subject had been broached, she waited while Pamela checked the phone.

"It's the sheriff's department. I'd better take it." Pamela answered the phone, then listened, her eyes widening as the caller spoke. "I'll be right there." She disconnected.

Before Kaylee could ask any questions, Giles emerged from the back. "I'm sorry, Mrs. Smythe. Where were we?"

Pamela launched herself to her feet with a tiny grunt. "I'll be back later. Someone broke into my house and I need to go see what's missing."

The funeral director's mouth gaped open in surprise, but he recovered himself quickly. "Anytime you want to come back, ma'am. We'll be ready to serve you." He hurried ahead and opened the front door.

"Which deputy called?" Kaylee asked Pamela as she followed her outside, an idea percolating in her mind.

"The handsome one. Deputy Durham." Pamela hopped inside her red truck and started the engine.

Kaylee dug for her phone and called Nick. When he answered, she said without preamble, "I've identified that seed. When should I drop by to tell you about it?" Or at least that was her angle. Wilfred's office and David's house had both been broken into within twenty-four hours. That couldn't possibly be a coincidence.

"Why don't you swing by Pamela Smythe's? A neighbor let her dog out this morning and saw the back door hanging open. So she called us." He gave her the address, which was in a neighborhood of older homes close to downtown. "See you in a few."

Kaylee gave Mary a call before leaving the funeral chapel. "I'm going to swing by the Smythe house to see Nick for a minute," she told her assistant. "Then I'll be in."

"That's fine," Mary said. "Jessica brought over double chocolate scones so I've been properly fueled this morning. Bear has been a big help too."

Kaylee laughed. "Really?"

"Well, emotionally. He makes me feel better by being cute."

"I can't argue with that."

"Anyway, we only have a few orders to fill. Then we can get back to those wreaths."

The wreaths. Kaylee dragged in a breath. She kept forgetting about the Apple Fest, which was starting the day after tomorrow. At least they were sharing a booth with DeeDee and Jessica, which meant only a modest inventory from The Flower Patch was required, fewer items than if they were operating the booth alone.

"Why did we agree to do this again?" Kaylee joked.

Mary laughed. "You know why. It's a good cause and it helps the town."

"Oh, right. I'll be there soon." Cheered by the conversation, Kaylee hung up and started the SUV. No matter what else was going on, she had wonderful people in her life who always boosted her mood.

Using her GPS, Kaylee quickly found the Smythe home, which was even easier when she spotted the cruisers out front. The house was a compact, pale-green ranch, with an adjacent two-car garage and a small, neat yard.

Pamela had parked across the street and was striding toward the house when Kaylee pulled up. She waited, hands on hips, for Kaylee to climb out. "Did you follow me?" she demanded. The overly friendly and confiding manner of earlier had vanished.

Kaylee was taken aback by this change in attitude. "Of course not. I'm here to see Deputy Durham."

The widow gave a harrumph and stalked toward the house, frowning. Kaylee stayed a step or two behind her, letting her get there first. Pamela headed down a concrete path to a small brick patio in back, off of which a door leading into the house hung open.

This must be what the neighbor saw. Kaylee glanced to the left, where a similar house sat. Anyone who exited the back door there would have a perfect view of the Smythes' home and yard. In fact, as she studied the neighbor's house, she saw an older woman with short, permed hair standing on the deck and watching the proceedings.

"Pamela," the woman called, waving an arm. "Yoo-hoo!"

"Someone wants you," Kaylee said when Pamela ignored the summons.

Pamela curled her lip. "Ugh. Suzanne. The nosiest neighbor ever."

"She reported the break-in," Kaylee pointed out. Maybe Suzanne had seen something related to David's death. Nosy neighbors could be a blessing when it came to investigations.

"That's right, she did." Pamela waved to the woman. "I'll talk to you later, Suzanne. Right now I have to . . ." She motioned toward the house.

"Of course." Suzanne nodded her head, making her curls bounce. "I'll be here. Kettle's on." With that cheerful statement, she vanished into her house.

Kaylee stood back and allowed Pamela to cross the patio first.

The older woman stepped through the open door, then stopped short with an exclamation.

Peeking over Pamela's shoulder, Kaylee saw the cause of her distress. The kitchen had been turned upside down. Cupboard doors stood open, their contents—food and dishes both—scattered over the countertops, table, and floor. The refrigerator and freezer doors hung open too, and whatever had been in there had been dumped on top of the disorder, adding to the mess. A river of melted ice cream snaked under the table, where chairs lay on their sides.

Deputies Durham and Brooks stood in a clear spot taking pictures and making notes. "Mrs. Smythe," Nick said. "This is how we found the place."

Pamela took a cautious step inside, her boot heel crunching on broken glass. "This isn't how we normally leave it, I assure you. David was a slob but he didn't do this."

"There are a couple of possibilities here," Nick said. "One is that someone was angry and vandalized the place. The other is that they were looking for something."

Kaylee's gaze met Nick's, and she could tell he shared her thoughts. The same thing had happened at Wilfred's, which led her to surmise that his second suggestion was more likely.

Pamela ran a hand through her hair. "I can't imagine who would trash the place. We didn't keep anything of value here." She snorted. "The most valuable thing we own is the Beechcraft, and that's at the airport."

The airplane David was selling. "That's a very nice airplane," Kaylee commented, hoping to learn more.

"It belonged to my father." Pamela curled her lip. "David wanted to sell it so we'd have more cash for the development. Engineers and site plans cost a lot."

"And you didn't agree?" Nick asked smoothly.

"What?" Pamela took a step back, a hand to her chest. "What

are you implying?" Bright spots appeared in her cheeks. "You think I killed my husband for the *airplane*? It already belonged to me."

Alan put up a hand. "Hold on, Mrs. Smythe. We weren't accusing you of anything."

Nick cleared his throat. "I'm just trying to get a full picture, ma'am." He gestured. "I need to show you something else."

The women picked their way through the debris after the officers, trying to avoid the worst of the chaos. Durham and Brooks halted in the doorway of a room adjacent to the kitchen. In addition to a big-screen television and leather sofa and chair, the room held a desk, file cabinet, and bookshelves. As in Wilfred's office, papers were strewn everywhere.

"I don't understand," the widow said, staring in dismay. "What could there possibly be in our paperwork that anyone would want?"

"That's a good question," Nick said. "Why don't you check and see if something's missing? The same in the kitchen."

Pamela muttered under her breath, obviously not happy at the prospect of the work ahead. She stomped back into the kitchen, heedless of what she was stepping on—or in. A few splotches of melted ice cream dotted the floor, left behind by her boots.

As Kaylee followed, walking more carefully, she spotted a red-and-yellow package lying between the refrigerator and the adjacent cabinet. Something about it rang a bell.

"What is it, Kaylee?" Nick asked, stopping behind her.

Kaylee pointed. "Can you get that out of there?"

"I'll do it." Alan used a broom handle to tease the small box out of its space. Once it was free, he peered closely at it. "It's rat poison," he said, surprise coloring his voice.

"Better take it into evidence," Nick said. "And use gloves."

Pamela crunched back to Kaylee's side and gaped at the package, then the deputies. "I've never seen that before in my life."

9

The deputies regarded Pamela with skepticism. "Are you absolutely sure about that, ma'am?" Nick asked. "Many people do keep rodent poison around."

Pamela stomped her foot, her hands fisted. "Yes I am. We don't have mice in this house, let alone rats. Someone planted that here."

Kaylee frowned, deep in thought. Instead of coming to the Smythes' to steal something, had the intruder tried to implicate Pamela? The burglar could have ransacked the home to cover their tracks.

"We can probably get prints," Alan said. "If it belongs to the Smythes, their fingerprints will be on it."

"Go ahead. You won't find mine on there," Pamela said, tossing her hair defiantly.

Nick rested his hands on his hips. "Why don't you and I take a walk-through, Mrs. Smythe, while Deputy Brooks takes our discovery into evidence? I want to make sure nothing else is out of place."

"Or that we don't find something else that doesn't belong here?" Pamela suggested. "Fine."

Kaylee checked the time and grimaced. "Before you do that, may I have a word, Deputy?"

"Sure," Nick said. "Let's go out to the patio."

Once outside, alone except for Suzanne making periodic forays onto her deck, Kaylee shared the results of her lab work.

"So that plant is pretty rare in the islands?" Nick sounded amazed at the break. "Good work, Kaylee."

"I think you need to check David's logbook," Kaylee said,

lowering her voice. "Since he owns an airplane, he probably flew to one of those islands."

Nick gazed around the yard, thinking. When his eyes fell on Suzanne, she yelped and vanished inside her house. "I love it when I have that effect on people," he said with a grin. "You're right about the logbook. I'll get a search warrant for the plane ASAP."

"I appreciate you doing that," Kaylee said. Even though the case against Wilfred looked open and shut, the department was still investigating. The discovery of poison here also cast doubt on Wilfred, at least in Kaylee's eyes. "About that poison—"

Nick shook his head. "I really can't talk about it, but I will say this: If that package had been in the house when we first searched, we would have found it."

"I'm sure. So the question is, who put it there? Pamela or the intruder?"

The deputy turned toward the door. "Time will tell. Have a good day, Kaylee. And thanks again."

"Let me know if you need anything else."

Nick paused. "Actually, could you please drop that evidence folder back at the station for me?"

"Sure." Kaylee headed across the grass, eager to get on with her day.

"Yoo-hoo!" Suzanne from next door hailed her.

Kaylee's steps hitched. She really ought to go—but maybe Suzanne had seen something notable. She pivoted and crossed the grass to the neighbor's yard. "Hi," she said. "I don't think we've met. I'm Kaylee Bleu."

Suzanne nodded, making her curls tremble. "I know who you are. You own the flower shop. I've also heard that you solve mysteries."

Kaylee laughed. "Don't let the deputies hear you say that."

Suzanne leaned against the deck rail with both hands. "Well, once in a while they need a helping hand. They're only human, after all." She nibbled her bottom lip, a furrow appearing between her brows. "Maybe you can give me some advice."

"I'll try."

"It's just . . . sometimes you see something, or hear something, and it bothers you, but you don't think anything of it until—"

"Until something bad happens?" Kaylee guessed.

"That's right. Something bad." Again, Suzanne worried at her poor lip. "The night before David died, he had a visitor. Not that I always notice, but I was sitting out here since it was such a warm night."

"David had a visitor?" Kaylee reiterated.

"Yes. It was dark so I didn't see him too clearly. But I got the impression he was young. He had crazy hair." She wiggled her fingers on top of her head to demonstrate. "Even curlier than mine."

Brett Horne. That didn't surprise Kaylee, since Brett and David were partners in the fly-in community development. But something about the visit must have bothered Suzanne, or else why mention it?

"I think I know who you mean," Kaylee said cautiously. "Go on."

"The two of them were sitting out on the patio, talking. I really didn't pay attention until the young one raised his voice. He said"—here she deepened her voice in imitation—"'I had major reservations about working with you after what happened in Seattle, Smythe.' He gave a nasty laugh, then said, 'I'm putting you on notice. You've messed with me for the last time.' It was strange, to say the least."

Kaylee's pulse quickened. She'd heard Lorraine imply that Brett Horne had some kind of negative history with David. And now it sounded like the younger man had threatened his business partner the day before he died. "You should tell the deputies what you heard, Suzanne," she urged.

Suzanne put a hand to her mouth, her eyes gleaming with excitement. "You really think it might have a bearing on the case? I mean, I wondered after I heard they arrested Wilfred, not that I believe he's guilty of murder. Such a sweet man."

"I'm not sure if what you heard is important," Kaylee said, "but it might well be." She stepped closer. "One more thing. I'm really glad you confided in me, but don't tell anyone else besides the police, okay?" She was thinking especially of Pamela, who might visit her neighbor. "We don't want to jeopardize the investigation."

"I won't, I promise. And I'll go over right away. Well, after Pamela leaves. Or if she comes here like she said, I'll call the station later. Thank you so much, Kaylee."

"Glad I could be of help." Kaylee strode off toward her vehicle, reflecting that she really hadn't done anything except listen. But perhaps a listening ear was all people needed sometimes.

After stopping by the sheriff's department office to return the silverpuff seeds to custody, Kaylee drove back to Turtle Cove. By the time she entered The Flower Patch, she felt as though she hadn't been there in days.

Bear ran to greet her, his claws skittering on the polished floor. "I'm happy to see you too, buddy." Kaylee bent to ruffle his silky head and ears.

"So tell me all," Mary said, setting a fresh mug of coffee on the counter. "I understand from DeeDee that you guys had a little excitement last night."

Kaylee gave Bear a final pat and went to the counter to drink her coffee. "We sure did. And it was thanks to this brave boy right here that we even knew someone broke in." As Kaylee sipped the hot, rich brew, she took Mary through the sequence of events the previous night and the present day so far. Although she'd suggested that Suzanne keep Brett's threat to herself, she knew she could trust Mary.

"I hope Suzanne does report what she heard," Mary said. "It might be enough for reasonable doubt. And what do you suppose that rat poison is about? How strange."

"It sure is." Kaylee finished off her coffee. "I've never heard of an intruder dropping something off."

"Me neither," Mary said. "What puzzles me nearly as much is what those silverpuff seeds have to do with the case, if anything."

"You and me both." Kaylee knew that the seeds could easily prove to be a wild-goose chase.

The shop doorbell jingled and Reese walked in. "Good afternoon, ladies."

"Is it afternoon?" Kaylee glanced at the clock. "No wonder my belly is rumbling. I'm starving."

"You've been running like a madwoman," Mary said, then pointed toward the kitchen. "You'll find a slow cooker of meatball soup in there. Plus homemade bread."

At Mary's words, Kaylee's stomach ramped up operations. "Yum. Want some, Reese?"

"I never say no to Mary's cooking," the handyman replied. "Then I'll get to work on the outside light." At Kaylee's puzzled expression, he added, "One of the spotlights is out. Mary called me about it."

"The socket must be loose," Mary said. "The bulb is new."

"You called the right man for the job," Kaylee said. "Come on back to the kitchen, Reese."

They went to the kitchen, Bear following close behind. As Kaylee pulled the lid off the slow cooker, she inhaled the welcome aroma of broth. She ladled out two bowls of soup and handed them to Reese to put on the small table. Then she sliced a few pieces of bread while he located butter in the refrigerator.

The pair sat down to eat, digging in with murmurs of appreciation. After a few bites, Kaylee set her spoon in her bowl. "Want to hear the updates? I'm warning you—we might be here a while."

Reese's eyes crinkled as he smiled. "You bet. I heard a little through the grapevine. Namely Jess, when I stopped by the café for coffee this morning."

Kaylee realized she hadn't seen Reese since Wilfred's arrest. "The most important development is that Wilfred got out on bail this morning."

"That's one of the updates I heard." Reese reached for another slice of bread. "I'm so relieved. Now we need to figure out who the real killer is."

"Exactly." Kaylee told Reese about her identification of the seeds, the break-ins at the farm and David's house, and the discovery of another package of poison in the Smythes' kitchen.

Reese's handsome face revealed his bemusement. "Talk about muddying the waters. If it's the same stuff that was at Wilfred's, then which package was used to kill David?"

"That's the million-dollar question. I also have no idea how the forensics team will answer it." If they couldn't, then it might be enough to raise reasonable doubt about Wilfred's guilt.

"Tyler Stevens is going to chew up the DA over this one." Reese grinned confidently. "They might even drop the charges."

"That would be great, but I want Wilfred to be completely cleared." Kaylee pondered how they could pinpoint the real culprit. "What stumps me is how and when David's coffee could have been doctored. There's an awful lot of activity at the FBO. People are in and out constantly."

He leaned back in his chair and folded his arms. "Seriously. What did someone do, lurk and wait for David to leave it unattended? That's highly unlikely." Then light broke over his features. "I know what happened."

10

"Well, don't leave me hanging. What?" Kaylee demanded.

Reese leaned forward, his expression eager. "Someone swapped David's thermos for one doctored with poison."

Kaylee's pulse leaped. She could picture the whole thing. "I saw the thermos. It was one of those stainless steel ones everyone has." She named the brand. "It would be really easy to do that. So the full thermos is sitting in his kitchen or at the FBO, the way it did every morning. The killer swaps them out at an opportune moment."

Reese picked up the tale. "Later on, he pours a cup and drinks, but by the time he notices something off about the taste—if he did—it's too late."

"Wow. It all fits." Kaylee's mind clicked into gear. If the thermos tampering had happened at home, then Pamela and Brett were the likeliest candidates, although Wilfred's fingerprint was a mystery in that case. At the FBO, Brett was still a leading contender—and so was Wilfred. But so were quite a few other people, since it was a public place.

They'd figured out an important clue, but they still had a long way to go before the mystery was solved.

"By the way," Reese said. "I have a flying lesson tomorrow morning. Want to meet me at the airport before we go up? We can talk to Wilfred about all this."

She heard his unspoken suggestion loud and clear. *And do some more investigating around the FBO.* "I'd love to."

In the morning, Kaylee loaded a canopy tent, a folding table, and chairs into the shop's delivery van, figuring she might as well set up the shared Apple Fest booth after she met with Reese and Wilfred. The event was kicking off the next day, and she and Mary would bring over their inventory then, as would Jessica and DeeDee. She decided to bring Bear along instead of leaving him with Mary. The airport was dog-friendly, and she hated to deprive him of an excursion.

The airport parking lot was almost full, and judging by the number of people unloading vehicles, other vendors had the same idea as Kaylee. On the tarmac, white tents were popping up one by one. Fly-in activities were underway, with a class for pilots in the FBO and several planes taking off and landing.

Reese had sent a text telling her to meet him by the concessions tent, located on the tarmac near the FBO. She found Reese and Wilfred standing out of the flow of foot traffic, chatting and sipping from paper cups of coffee. Under the tent, cooks flipped pancakes and tended sizzling sausage links and bacon while customers lined up to buy breakfast.

Kaylee's belly rumbled. She'd had only coffee before leaving the house. "Good morning," she called as she approached. Bear ran toward the men, tags jingling and tail wagging, until he reached the end of his leash and had to wait for Kaylee to catch up.

The men said hello, then Reese asked, "Can I get you a coffee and something to eat? They're selling pretty good apple coffee cake." He winked. "I think it was made by a friend of ours."

A piece of Jessica's coffee cake would definitely hold Kaylee until lunch. "Coffee and cake sounds perfect. Thanks." As Reese hurried off, Kaylee smiled at an older couple pausing to admire Bear. The woman crouched down to pat his head and coo endearments, which the little dog enjoyed immensely.

"Beautiful day to fly," Kaylee commented to Wilfred after the couple wandered off.

Wilfred craned his head to peer at the clear blue sky. "Sure is." He sighed deeply. "I'm in full appreciation of the privilege, believe me."

Kaylee could understand his sentiments. Even the thought of being locked away from all she cherished made her shudder, and this poor man was staring that very real possibility in the face. For someone who enjoyed the freedom of the open skies, the prospect of jail time and having his pilot's license revoked must be torture.

A familiar figure came charging across the tarmac. Kaylee could practically feel the intensity in Jocko's eyes. "Wilfred, you may want to brace yourself," Kaylee warned. "Here comes a reporter."

The older man took her literally, moving his legs to a wide stance and folding his arms across his chest as the other man reached them. "I don't have anything to say, young feller," he told Jocko.

Jocko cocked his head, his bright eyes inquisitive. "Are you sure about that? I'd love to hear your side of the story. Drum up some public sympathy and all." When Wilfred didn't reply, Jocko glanced behind him to watch an airplane taking off. "Are you going up in your plane today? Must be a relief the judge said you could." He faced them again. "What's your destination?"

"Jocko, how do you expect anyone to take you seriously when you keep acting like a paparazzo? I thought you wanted to be a legitimate journalist," Kaylee said. She'd first met the young reporter lurking around a movie set, trying to land a hot story to sell to the tabloids.

He beamed at her, shaking his straw-like hair out of his

eyes. "And legitimate journalists ask the tough questions. The ones other people are afraid to. Listen, I'm only trying to help."

Carrying a paper coffee cup and a bakery bag, Reese re-joined them. "Are you bothering my friends, Jocko? Why don't you give it a rest?"

"Well, hi, Reese," Jocko returned brightly. "I never bother people. But my reporter's instincts never rest, so how can I? Are you sure you don't want to make a statement, Mr. Bates? The story will run anyway."

"I'm certain we can trust you for fair and accurate reporting," Kaylee said with a smile. "Right, Jocko?"

"Of course," the young man returned. "How could you ever think otherwise?" Something behind them seemed to catch his eye. "Excuse me. I need to talk to Mr. Horne over there." He trotted away.

"On to a new victim," Wilfred said. "Let's take a walk over to my hangar." He pointed toward a row of similar buildings built with wide doors facing the runway. "Mine is the pale green one in the middle."

The group strolled along the tarmac, admiring the airplanes they passed. Kaylee knew almost nothing about their makes and models, but she enjoyed viewing the sleek, colorful aircraft.

When they reached Wilfred's hangar, he unlocked a padlock and pushed the door up, revealing the plane Kaylee had seen Reese landing.

"Climb inside if you want," Wilfred said, his face shining with pride. "Cherokee 180. She's my baby. I did the whole restoration myself." Pictures on the walls showed the plane before and after Wilfred's work, which included a shiny new paint job.

"Wilfred is an A&P mechanic," Reese explained.

"A&P?" Kaylee asked.

Reese smiled. "It stands for Airframe and Powerplant."

The pilot adjusted his ball cap with a laugh. "And it means I can earn a few bucks to support my flying habit by working on planes. Plus I keep my craft airworthy myself. That saves money too."

Kaylee peered through the pilot's window at the array of instruments on the panel. It all seemed very complicated, but no doubt once you learned what they all meant, they made sense.

Reese unlatched the door. "Want to get in?"

Bear pranced and whined at his words, and they all laughed. "Is he allowed inside?" Kaylee asked. "His nails are clipped, so he won't scratch the leather upholstery. He's also not a chewer."

"He'd probably be the first dog in my plane, but he's welcome," Wilfred said.

Kaylee climbed inside and slipped in a passenger seat, placing Bear on her lap, and the two pilots sat up front. They sipped coffee while Reese gave Kaylee a verbal tour of the panel under Wilfred's watchful eye. Some of the instruments indicated the position and speed of the aircraft while others told the pilot how the engine was performing.

"And that very important indicator tells us if we have enough fuel," Reese concluded, pointing at the gauge.

"Too many accidents are due to foolishly running out of gas," Wilfred said, shaking his head dolefully. "Never let yourself get overconfident, Reese. That's when you make mistakes."

"Yes sir." Reese's expression was solemn, and Kaylee sensed he was absorbing the older pilot's wisdom like a sponge. "I've done that before, in my own work. But a mistake thousands of feet in the air is a little harder to come back from."

"That's for sure." Wilfred stared out the windshield, watching a plane taxi along the runway. As it lifted off, he sighed deeply. "I understand you wanted to talk to me, Kaylee?"

Kaylee took a moment to organize her thoughts. She wasn't

sure if Wilfred's attorney knew about the new evidence, so she decided not to mention that yet. But since sheriff department calls were public record, she started by asking, "Did you hear that someone broke into David Smythe's house?"

"DeeDee told me," the older man said. "I thought it a strange coincidence that my place and David's were both broken into around the same time."

"Me too," Kaylee said. "I wonder what they were looking for." *Or leaving behind, perhaps.*

"After DeeDee dropped me off yesterday, I said hello to the animals and then cleaned up my office." Wilfred paused. "Only one file was missing, as far as I can tell."

Kaylee's heart skipped a beat. Maybe they were finally getting a break. Reese sent her a significant glance, his brows raised. Then he asked, "Which file?"

Wilfred cleared his throat. His gaze was locked on the dash, but Kaylee suspected he wasn't really seeing it. "My friend Don Heaton loaned me some money a few months ago. Now I can't find the paperwork."

"Forgive me, but are you sure?" Reese asked.

"Absolutely," Wilfred said adamantly, then chuckled. "My files have never been so organized."

Kaylee wondered why someone would take those particular documents. Even with them gone, Wilfred still owed the money. And Don of course would have a copy.

A tiny alarm rang in the back of her mind but she brushed it aside. Her imagination must be running away with her.

She remembered the conversation she'd overheard between Wilfred and David. "Wilfred, the other night after the vendor meeting, I wasn't trying to eavesdrop, but I heard David talking about taking your land."

"Oh, that." Wilfred was silent for a long moment. Kaylee

hoped she hadn't overstepped by mentioning what she'd heard, but she needed to know more about the relationship between the two men if she was going to help.

"Are you okay, Wilfred?" Reese asked.

Nodding, Wilfred rearranged his ball cap on his head, a familiar gesture. "David was always after me to sell to him. When I kept saying no, I guess he thought he'd resort to threats."

"Unless he did have some kind of leverage," Reese said. "Like that loan."

Wilfred frowned. "I don't see how—" He broke off and dug for the cell phone in his pocket. "I'm going to give Don a call." He punched in the number and listened. "He didn't pick up, but his cell signal can be a bit weak out there. I'll try again later. Or maybe we'll just fly over to see him."

"Where does he live?" Kaylee asked.

"On his own little island," Wilfred replied. "It's a fun, if short, hop."

"Maybe you can come along," Reese said to Kaylee with a grin. "The plane has four seats, as you noticed."

"I'd love to go," Kaylee said, pleased with the invitation. "Let me know when and I'll try to come."

Kaylee left the pilots to their preflight checklist, and she and Bear made their way back to the parking lot. As she was unloading on the tarmac, she saw Wilfred and Reese take off. She stopped to watch as the red-and-white plane lifted from the ground and soared into the blue.

The vendor next to her, an older woman Kaylee didn't recognize, was also watching the Cherokee. She brayed a laugh. "That's the last we'll see of Wilfred, I bet. He's probably headed right to Canada." She reached into a box and pulled out a handful of the plastic bracelets she was selling.

Kaylee tried to suppress her irritation but she felt she had to respond. "Actually, Wilfred is giving my friend a lesson." She noticed the acid in her tone and tried to cover it with a laugh. "They'd better come back. Reese is supposed to do some work for me at my shop."

The woman dumped the bracelets on her table, staring at Kaylee with her mouth hanging open. With a huff, she turned her back and began hanging up the trinkets on a flimsy stand. Another vendor came over, and the two began to whisper, stealing furtive glances at Kaylee as they did. The occasional word she overheard was enough to tell her they were talking about Wilfred and his alleged guilt.

Kaylee tried to focus on setting up the tent, which fought her every step of the way. But her thoughts went around in circles as she mulled over the case. They had to clear Wilfred. The poor man was certainly brave to show his face at the airport. No doubt the gossipy bracelet woman was only one of many who believed in his guilt.

A sheriff's cruiser drove slowly along the edge of the tarmac, Nick at the wheel and Alan riding shotgun. The ladies at the next booth noticed and their whispering ratcheted up a notch. When Nick parked by one of the larger hangars, Kaylee realized he was probably taking her advice and checking David's plane for the seeds.

Her suspicions were confirmed when Brett strode across the tar toward the hangar, unlocked the door, and disappeared inside with both deputies.

Kaylee abandoned the tent, which was standing crooked, and headed over with Bear. As the botanical forensics expert, she had a role in the investigation. And sometimes that role came in handy.

As she reached the open door, Brett came out. "Hey, Kaylee." She couldn't help but think of what David's neighbor had overheard. Was Brett the killer? "How are you, Brett?" Kaylee halted, tugging at the lead as Bear trotted toward the manager.

"Good," he replied, glancing around, his posture tense and fists clenched at his sides. "Busy day." He sent Bear a wan smile as the dog sniffed his shoes.

"Very busy. I'm in the middle of setting up our booth." Kaylee moved to a more comfortable stance. "Are you ready for the Apple Fest tomorrow?"

"Ready as I'll ever be," he said, still appearing distracted. Did he have a lot on his mind or did he simply not want to talk to her? "Well, I—"

"I ran into Pamela at the funeral chapel." Kaylee shook her head sadly. "Poor thing. She's devastated."

Now his gaze met hers, brows raised. "She is? Uh, I mean, of course." He shifted his attention away from Kaylee. "It's a loss, truly. Place won't be the same."

"Are you going ahead with the development, do you think?" Kaylee whistled to Bear, who was now sniffing around a trash can. She glanced back at Brett in time to see a strange smile on his face.

He quickly straightened his features. "Probably." He rubbed the back of his neck. "Pamela wants to. They planned to live in one of the units." His lips clamped shut as if he realized he was saying too much. Darting another glance toward the FBO, he began walking. "I'd better get back. See you later."

Kaylee watched him stride away. Something was up with Brett. He was edgy, evasive, distracted. In other words, definitely still on the suspect list—in her eyes anyway.

After tying Bear to a post so he wouldn't disturb the scene, she entered the hangar. The deputies were crawling around inside the Beechcraft, doing their best to search a cramped area. Kaylee waited until Nick was near the door and glanced her way.

"Find anything interesting?" she asked. David's plane was

a beauty, larger than the Cherokee with paint that gleamed.

"Not yet," Nick said. "We just got started."

"Here's more of those seed things," Alan called, his voice muffled because his upper half was in the cockpit.

"I stand corrected," Nick said. "We did find something. You can take them now and see if they're a match."

Kaylee nodded. "Of course." She had no doubt the seeds would match the others, but of course they needed to be absolutely sure. Then they needed to link David's flight schedule to where the plants were found. "Are there any logbooks? They should be there somewhere."

"That's right, the logbooks. Brett said there should be David's pilot log and the plane's log," Nick said. He disappeared deeper into the plane, searching through the aircraft cabin. A few minutes later he reappeared. "I can't find them anywhere. They're missing."

11

"Are you sure?" Kaylee asked. Her heart sank at this news, although she wasn't totally surprised. If someone had taken the records to hide information about where David had flown, then it was even more critical that they were located.

"Yes, unfortunately," Nick replied. "I double-checked every-where, even under the seats."

"I didn't see any logbooks either," Alan added.

Kaylee glanced around the hangar and noticed a desk in one corner. "Maybe they're over there."

"We'd better check right now." Nick sighed. "This case is really something. Evidence is either being added or removed from the scenes."

Kaylee stepped closer to the plane, wanting to check out the plush interior. "Do you think the poison was left at David's by the intruder?"

"Possibly," Nick said. "We didn't find any prints. If David or Pamela had bought it for the house, they surely would have left some."

"It's those crime shows," Alan called out. "Everyone knows to wear gloves now."

Kaylee pictured someone wearing gloves at the store where the poison was purchased. But then there would be prints from the cashier. "Or they wiped the box clean."

Nick exited the aircraft and went over to the desk. He searched among the folders and papers on top and through the side drawers. "Nothing," he said with disgust. "Someone must have walked off with those logbooks."

"Ask his wife," Kaylee said. "Maybe she took them to show someone." At Nick's questioning look, she added, "The plane is for sale. I saw the poster in the FBO."

"How much?" Kaylee named the price, and the deputy whistled. "Why do you think he was selling? To fund the development?"

"Maybe," Kaylee said. "Or perhaps he was going to trade this one in. Pamela can probably answer that question."

"Did I hear my name?" Pamela Smythe marched into the hangar, heels clicking. "But first, tell me what you're all doing in here."

"We have a search warrant." Nick held it out to her. "The manager let us in. He said this hangar belongs to the airport."

Pamela glanced over the warrant. "It does. Plant debris? Why do you need that?"

"We're trying to track David's recent flights," Nick said. "But I have a question for you. Have you seen David's logbooks?"

Bright spots appeared on Pamela's cheeks. "No." Her tone was offended. "They're supposed to stay with the airplane at all times. David flew this plane recently, so his should be in there."

"Well, nothing is in the plane now," Nick said, then pointed to the desk he stood beside. "And nothing here either."

Pamela bustled toward the airplane, waving her hand at Alan, who had appeared in the doorway. "If you're done, get out of there. I need to find those logbooks."

The deputy clambered down, clutching the evidence envelope.

While Pamela dug through the cockpit, Nick said, "I understand you're trying to sell this airplane."

Her head rose into view, her blonde locks disarranged by the search. "David wanted to sell, but I'm taking it off the market. This plane belonged to my dad." She disappeared again, faint grunts and exclamations drifting toward Kaylee and the deputies.

Would anyone keep a plane for sentimental reasons, especially one so valuable? Kaylee thought of something. "Pamela, do you fly?" she called.

As if she hadn't heard, Pamela made her way back to the hangar floor. "Nothing." Her tone was disgusted. "If I find out who—" Then Kaylee's question seemed to sink in. Pamela cocked her head. "As a matter of fact, I do. I actually have more hours than my husband."

"More hours?" Alan asked. "What does that mean?"

Pamela ran a hand over her hair, trying to pat it back into place. "In their logbooks, pilots track hours flown plus the aircraft they were flying and, in some cases, the type of maneuvers they did. They are proof of your experience and ability."

"So where's your logbook?" Nick asked.

The woman's eyes slid toward the hangar entrance then back to Nick. "I took it home." A smile curved her lips. "If you want to see it, you'll need another warrant." She crossed her arms. "But I haven't been flying lately. My medical ran out and I haven't gotten a new one." It was another unfamiliar flying term. Pamela seemed to notice their confusion, because she added in exasperation, "With my type of license, I need to have a current physical. Okay? Are we done here?"

A few minutes later they exited the hangar, Kaylee with more questions than when she went inside. Missing logbooks, Pamela a licensed pilot, the silverpuff seeds—what did it all mean? Maybe nothing. Possibly everything.

After finishing her booth setup, Kaylee stopped by the funeral chapel and determined that the seeds were indeed a match to the ones in David's cuff. Next, she and Bear swung by the sheriff's department to drop off the evidence, and then they returned to Turtle Cove.

Mary was hanging out the *Open* sign in front of The Flower Patch. "Good morning, Kaylee." She studied her boss a little more closely. "You look tired. Bad night?"

Kaylee laughed as she let Bear off his leash. "No, hectic morning." While Mary watered the hanging plants and containers accenting the Victorian-style porch, she filled her in.

"Wow, you have been busy." Mary drained the watering can. "I think we need coffee and a muffin." She reached into the pocket of her apron and pulled out her wallet. "Want to pop over to Death by Chocolate for us?"

Kaylee had already eaten coffee cake that morning—but surely she'd burned off those calories by now, she decided. "That sounds perfect." She waved a hand at Mary's wallet. "Keep that. It's my treat."

Bear trotted inside with Mary, and Kaylee walked next door.

"Hello, stranger," Jessica greeted her from behind the counter. "What's up?"

Kaylee sighed. "I don't even know where to begin." She pointed to the pumpkin chocolate chip muffins. "I'll take two of those."

Jessica pulled a square of paper from a dispenser and used it to grab the muffins. "DeeDee has been keeping me posted, more or less." She glanced around the bakery, which was experiencing a rare lull. "But I'm all ears for anything you want to tell me."

"I only have time to tell you the highlights." Kaylee placed the rest of their order, then gave her friend a brief rundown of the past several days. "The most exciting thing is I could get to go flying with Wilfred and Reese. Wilfred might be visiting a friend on an outlying island."

"Really?" Jessica clasped her hands together in supplication. "Can

I come? Pretty please? I've been dying to go up in a small plane."

The Cherokee had four seats, so Kaylee didn't see a problem with her coming along, but it was up to the pilot. "Let me check, okay?"

"Sure thing," Jessica said with a smile.

Kaylee checked her phone and saw that she'd somehow missed a call. After she saw the caller identification, she said, "You won't believe it. I think Kip just called me."

"Kip?" Jessica's forehead creased. "Someone I should know?"

"Kip Bates," Kaylee said. "Wilfred's son." Frankly, she'd forgotten all about him. "I'd better call him back."

Jessica slapped her forehead. "Oh, *that* Kip. Go on, call him."

Kaylee grabbed her purchases and edged toward the door, her mind already on the call. "I will, as soon as I step outside."

"And don't forget to let me know about going flying."

"I won't. Promise." With a laugh, Kaylee scooted out of the bakery. After climbing the steps onto The Flower Patch's porch, she set down the muffins and coffee cups, then perched on a rocker to call Kip back.

"Kip Bates here." His voice was low in volume yet confident. In the background, Kaylee heard the clacking of keys and other voices in the background. He must be at work.

"Kip, this is Kaylee Bleu."

"Ms. Bleu, I'll save you some time. I saw the news, which mentioned that my father had been arrested for . . . murder." The confidence wavered.

Now that she'd found Wilfred's son, Kaylee felt a pang of trepidation. Here she was, talking to a stranger about his father. A stranger who had—according to DeeDee—deliberately stayed out of touch with Wilfred. She should have had DeeDee make the call, since she knew the Bates men. *Too late for that.*

"He's innocent, Kip." As the words burst out, Kaylee was vaguely aware she had used his first name, despite his calling her Ms. Bleu. "My friends and I are trying to clear him. Oh, and he's out on bail, which is great."

He chuckled. "You and your friends? What are you? An Orcas Island Nancy Drew?"

Kaylee's cheeks heated, but she stayed focused. "Some evidence has come up that points away from your father." Which direction wasn't yet clear, but it was away from Wilfred, fortunately.

"That's good to hear." He sighed. "What exactly did you need from me, Ms. Bleu?"

"I guess . . . well, DeeDee Wilcox, your dad's goddaughter, thought you should know. Maybe you could call or visit to give him support." Even though her parents lived in Florida, Kaylee knew they'd hurry here to help her. And vice versa.

A long silence followed. Kaylee stared at DeeDee's bookstore across the street, wanting more than anything to hand the phone over to her. Once she'd found Kip's number, she should have asked DeeDee to call instead of jumping the gun.

Kip sighed again. "I'll see what I can do about coming to the island."

Yes! Kaylee pumped her fist, which earned a narrow gaze from walkers passing by. She grinned at them.

"But don't say anything to Dad, okay?" Kip asked. "I might not be able to get there for a bit." A shuffling sound came across the line. "I'm in the middle of a big project."

"I won't say a word," Kaylee promised. She paused, then added, "Maybe give him a call, though, if you think it will be a while. I'm sure he'd love to hear from you." She scrunched up her face, hoping she hadn't pushed too much.

Kip was quiet. "I'll think about it," he finally said. "Now I need to go. Have a good day."

As Kaylee hung up, the front door opened and Mary popped her head around the jamb. "Kaylee, did you get lost?"

Kaylee jumped up and gathered the coffee and muffins. "Sorry. Kip Bates left me a message so I returned his call."

Mary led the way inside. "I'll forgive you, as long as you tell me what he said."

"Of course." Kaylee's phone bleeped with a text. After setting down their snack on the counter, she pulled out her phone again.

It was a text from Reese. *Meet us at four. Destination: Hemlock Island.*

Hemlock Island. One of the sites where the rare silverpuff grew.

12

"Ready, ladies?" Wilfred greeted Kaylee and Jessica with a grin. The Cherokee was parked on the tarmac, doors open and ready to go. Reese was studying the preflight checklist.

Jessica wore an expression of wide-eyed excitement. "I've always wanted to take a flight over the island." She patted the camera she wore around her neck. "I'm hoping to get some great photos."

Kaylee wished she'd thought of that. But she was already carrying a tote with her magnifying glass, tweezers, and evidence bags so she could gather some silverpuff seeds. Maybe she could help prove that David Smythe had visited Hemlock Island.

Wilfred helped them into the airplane. The passenger area was compact, but they each had a window.

Kaylee found a spot for her tote and buckled the lap belt. Now that they were onboard, a rising sense of exhilaration fluttered in her belly. Unlike in an airliner, where the pilots were hidden from view, she and Jessica had practically a front-row seat to the entire operation.

After Wilfred and Reese climbed in, Reese gave them the required safety instructions regarding undoing the seat belts and the locations of the exits.

When Reese was done, Wilfred handed out headsets. "We'll be able to talk to each other with these. Otherwise it's quite noisy in here." He fired up the engine, filling the cockpit with a roar that made Kaylee's heart jump.

Once her headset was on, Kaylee noticed that it cut the drone of the engine quite a bit. "Can you hear me, Jess?"

"Sure can." Jessica grinned as the plane began to taxi.

The small craft raced down the runway and then lifted up into the air so gently that Kaylee didn't even feel it when their tires left the ground. The tarmac dropped away as they climbed toward the clouds.

"I never get tired of that feeling," Wilfred said. "Good job, Reese."

Reese is in command? Kaylee's heart gave a leap. She stole a glance at his profile, his expression intent as he checked the gauges and set their course. She wasn't surprised at his confidence. He always seemed competent at everything he did.

They circled over the airport and headed north, buildings and vehicles looking like toys below. Kaylee enjoyed the play of light and shadow over the rolling hills, and she even caught a glimpse of the tower on Mount Constitution.

Then they were over the water, waves rippling below, headed for Hemlock Island. More than 400 islands made up the San Juan archipelago, and only 172 of them had names. Even fewer of those were inhabited, and for those residents, boats or airplanes were the only way to or from their homes.

Hemlock Island was tiny, with only one house, a dock, and a grass strip to land on. Off to one side of the strip was a small airplane, which was parked next to a hangar.

"His Cessna is there, and so are his boats," Wilfred said, his voice crackling over the headset, "so Don should be home."

"Do you think someone picked him up?" Reese asked.

"That's a possibility, but then he'd be answering his phone," Wilfred replied. "I've tried him nearly a dozen times."

Reese lined up the aircraft with the runway and made the approach. Gusts of wind buffeted the plane as it descended, but Reese deftly adjusted to stay on course. Within a couple of minutes, they were on the ground and rolling to a stop.

"A1 landing." Wilfred clapped Reese on the shoulder, then

removed his headset. "Couldn't have done it better myself."

"That is high praise," Reese said, beaming. He twisted around in his seat. "How was it back there, ladies?"

"Awesome," Jessica said. "Will one of you take Luke and me up for a ride sometime?"

"Absolutely," Wilfred said. "I do scenic tours upon request."

After exiting the aircraft, Kaylee stood in the field and gazed at her surroundings, hearing the buzz of crickets in the grass. Now that they were on the ground, the air was still and she could hear waves rolling in to crash on the shore.

Wilfred pulled out his phone and dialed Don again. "He should have come right out when he heard us land," he fretted. He listened then disconnected. "Went to voice mail."

"The house is that way, right?" Reese asked, pointing to a break in the trees enclosing the field.

"Yes it is." Wilfred set off with his shoulders squared.

Reese and Jessica hurried to catch up, but Kaylee lingered to scan for silverpuff. It usually grew in wetter spots, so she searched for depressions in the landscape first.

There it was, near a patch of *Carex arcta*, a species of sedge. Kaylee set her tote beside the flowers and hurried to catch up to her friends. She'd gather specimens after they figured out whether Don was okay.

Kaylee crossed through a narrow band of woods and emerged into another clearing. The cedar house was large, built in a rustic style with overhangs that partially shaded the wraparound deck. Wilfred was knocking on the closest door while Jessica and Reese waited.

"Where were you?" Jessica asked.

"I stopped to hunt for a certain rare plant," Kaylee said as she tromped up the deck stairs. "I read that it grows on this island." She didn't want to say more in case Don Heaton was home and overheard.

But no one answered Wilfred's knocking. "Now what?"

"Try calling again," Reese said.

Wilfred pulled out his phone and dialed. A corresponding ringing sounded inside. Wilfred pocketed his phone. "Now we know his phone is in the house. But where is Don?"

Kaylee pressed her face to the glass, shading her hands. The others followed suit and, in that manner, they worked their way around the house.

But it was Kaylee who spotted the homeowner in the great room. Her heart sank when she saw a pair of legs in khaki pants on the floor, sticking out from behind a couch.

"Wilfred?" she called. "Can you tell if that's Don?" She stood aside so he could peer through the window.

Wilfred's face set in grim lines. "It's him all right. I recognize the shoes."

Reese tested the handle of a nearby French door. "Locked." He exchanged a glance with the other man. "We're going to have to break in."

At Wilfred's nod, Reese returned his focus to the door. "I'm not sure if kicking in the door or breaking the glass would be the better option," he said.

"What if we just tear out the screen on this window over here?" Jessica suggested. "The window is already open."

"I knew we brought you for a reason, Jess." Reese strode over to the window she'd indicated, then pulled out a pocket knife and sliced into the screen around the edges, creating an opening large enough to climb through. He dragged a bench over to give himself a boost, then hoisted himself up and into the house. A moment later, he appeared at the door, having unlocked it from the inside.

Wilfred, Jessica, and Kaylee rushed into the house. Reese hunkered down beside the unconscious Don, a stocky older man with a wide brow and disheveled silver hair. "He's breathing,"

Reese said. "His pulse is a little erratic but pretty strong."

"What do you think happened to him?" Jessica asked. She held a hand to her cheek, her dark eyes wide with concern.

Wilfred was already calling 911. "Don's been in poor health, nothing that would cause unconsciousness though. I wonder if it has to do with his medications." He pointed at an array of pill bottles on the breakfast bar, then spoke into the phone. "I'd like to report a medical emergency."

The nearest medical center was on Orcas Island. Kaylee stared out the huge windows at the magnificent view of water and distant islands. *Living here must be wonderful, except when something like this happens.*

"They're sending a chopper," Wilfred said after disconnecting the call. He began to pace back and forth, casting worried glances at his friend.

"Anyone want a glass of water?" Jessica asked. "I'm parched."

Kaylee followed her into the kitchen. "Don't touch anything, Jess." At her friend's confused expression, she explained, "Until we know what's wrong with Don, we'd better be careful."

Jessica backed away from the cabinets. "Are you thinking it was foul play?"

"I think we should be extra cautious." When Wilfred made the comment about the medication, Kaylee had accepted it at face value. But if David had come to see Don, maybe there was more to the situation than met the eye. And she couldn't forget that they were here because Wilfred's file about his loan from Don was missing.

Jessica seemed to accept this. "I'll run out to the plane and get my water bottle then."

Kaylee scanned the kitchen, which was immaculate. A fridge magnet caught her eye. *Deep Green Cleaning.* Another connection. "Look, Jess. Lorraine and maybe her son have been out here too."

Jessica studied the magnet with a frown. "That's not surprising, since Don is one of Wilfred's friends."

She was right, but Kaylee's instincts told her there might be more to learn. "I'll go out with you. I want to collect those samples."

Before leaving the house, Kaylee shared her theory with the men. "Until we know that what happened to Don isn't related to David's death, we'd better be careful not to contaminate evidence."

"Are you serious?" Wilfred's face darkened with anger as he stared down at Don's prone body. "Someone might have come in here and hurt Don on purpose?"

Reese pressed his lips together. "I agree with Kaylee, Wilfred. The theory is that David came out here, so maybe Don knows something about his murder."

Wilfred stared at the handyman in horror.

Kaylee wished she could make the distraught man feel better, but that wasn't likely to happen until his friend was out of the woods. Instead, she explained, "Silverpuff seeds were found in David's pant cuff and in his plane. His logbook is missing so it's all just speculation, but I think those seeds might match the plants I found in the field."

Wilfred cocked a brow. "His logbook is missing? That's serious business."

"I think someone was trying to hide the fact that David came out here," Kaylee said. "Or at least delay the sheriff's department from finding out."

"And now Don can't talk." Wilfred crouched and put a gentle hand on his friend's shoulder. "Hang in there, buddy. Help is on its way."

Kaylee realized Nick should be informed. She pulled out her cell phone and called him. Fortunately, he answered, and she gave him a brief rundown.

"You're doing the right thing," the deputy said. "I'll be over on a marine patrol boat shortly. Can you all wait for me?" When she confirmed that they could, he added, "Good job, Kaylee."

They hung up, and Kaylee turned to the others, "Nick will be here in a while. And he agrees that we need to treat this like a crime scene."

"I'm going out to get my water bottle," Jessica said. "Anyone else need something from the plane?"

"I'll take mine," Reese said. Wilfred echoed that.

"Be right back."

Jessica and Kaylee went out the door they'd come through so as not to leave prints elsewhere. Then the two women headed back through the woods to the field, scanning the sky for the medical chopper. A faint sound in the distance announced its pending arrival.

"Here's the silverpuff patch," Kaylee said, spotting her tote. "It should only take a couple of minutes for me to gather a sample."

Jessica stared at the plants. "It always amazes me how a seed, stem, or leaf can be used as proof in a criminal case. It's fascinating."

Kaylee laughed as she foraged for an evidence bag. "I'm glad I get to use my skills this way. It's a little more exciting than teaching." Granted, she had enjoyed sharing her love of botany with impressionable young minds.

While Kaylee gathered the seeds and Jessica dug in the cockpit, the whir of the chopper grew louder. Soon it was hovering overhead, the blades blowing the tall meadow grass almost flat.

Jessica returned from the Cherokee, bottles of water in hand, staring up at the helicopter as it descended. "Wow. That is really impressive."

Kaylee had to agree. The sheer power of the aircraft was awe-inspiring, the wind growing even stronger as it lowered to the ground. She quickly tucked the packet of seeds inside her bag before it could blow away.

The helicopter door opened and a couple of male para-medics—one with a crew cut and one with longish hair in a ponytail—emerged carrying a gurney.

"Where's the patient?" the medic with a crew cut called.

Kaylee pointed to the opening in the trees. "In the house."

"Let's head back," Jessica said after the paramedics disap-peared into the trees. "Maybe we can find out what's wrong with Don."

Inside the house, the EMTs examined Don, then moved him to the gurney, where they put an oxygen mask over his face. "Any idea what happened?" the one with a ponytail asked.

Wilfred explained that they'd found him in a coma, without any visible signs of injury or a fall. "He's on several medications," he said, indicating the pill bottles. "Maybe they had something to do with his condition."

The medic picked up a bottle and read the label. When it seemed as though he was going to take the medication along, Kaylee said, "Please leave those here. The sheriff's department is on their way."

"The sheriff's department?" A puzzled expression slid across the man's face. "You suspect foul play?" He frowned around at the immaculate room, which showed no signs of a struggle or disturbance.

"Maybe," Kaylee said. "Just being careful, since Mr. Heaton's illness may be related to a recent case."

The medic nodded. "I'll take your word for it. No point in getting Maddox riled up if we don't have to." He jotted down the doctor's name and the list of medications. "Let's go," he told his companion.

"Where are you taking him?" Wilfred asked.

"Seattle," the one with a crew cut said. He studied the

patient with compassionate eyes. "They're better equipped. Full hospital and all."

Wilfred swayed on his feet and Reese stepped to his side to support him. "Is he . . . going to make it?" Wilfred asked in a whisper.

"We'll do our best," the longhaired medic said. "You can be sure of that."

The foursome watched in somber silence as the paramedics rushed their charge out of the house. "He had to say that, you know," Jessica said, patting Wilfred's arm. "I'm sure Don will be fine."

"I know." Wilfred's voice was gruff. "But it doesn't make it any easier." He pulled a handkerchief out of his back pocket and wiped his face, then folded it neatly and tucked it away.

"Let's wait for Nick outside," Kaylee suggested. "He should be here any minute."

Bench seats lined the front deck, so they sat on those and sipped water, touched by rays from the setting sun. Kaylee wondered how long they'd be at the island and how they'd make it back in the dark.

"Don't worry." Reese must have noticed her squinting up at the evening sky. "Wilfred is licensed to fly with instruments."

The other pilot, who'd been sitting with head bowed and hands clasped between his knees, nodded.

"You read my mind," Kaylee said. "I was wondering about that." She spotted a boat moving fast toward the island, a wake creaming up on both sides. "Here comes the marine patrol."

The boat angled toward the dock, expertly cutting speed at the right time to slow and pull up alongside. The green-and-white boat was marked *Sheriff* in huge gold letters on the side.

"In case you weren't sure who they were," Reese said. The lame joke broke the tension a little.

Nick, Alan, and a couple of other deputies made their way

up to the house, carrying cases Kaylee recognized as evidence collection kits. They were taking her suspicions seriously.

Once the officers arrived on the deck, Nick greeted everyone, then asked, "What brought you out here today?"

"Don's a good friend of mine," Wilfred said. "In fact—" He slid his eyes to Kaylee, who nodded. Full transparency was best. "He loaned me money for my farm. When the loan paperwork went missing from my office, I called Don."

"Remember the prowler?" Kaylee put in. "The night DeeDee and I stayed at the farm? I think whoever that was took the file."

"Solid theory," Nick said. "So you followed up with Don, Wilfred?"

"I tried to," Wilfred said. "I called a bunch of times but didn't get an answer. I decided I'd better come check on him." He pointed a shaking finger toward the house. "And found him collapsed on the floor."

"He was unconscious so we called 911," Reese said. "The EMTs are taking him to a Seattle hospital. Wilfred thought maybe it had something to do with Don's medications. He's on quite a few."

"Did you touch anything inside?" Nick asked.

They all shook their heads, Jessica sending Kaylee a relieved look.

"Good. We're going to go in and check things out. Why don't you wait here?"

While Kaylee, Jessica, Reese, and Wilfred sat on the benches on the deck, Nick put the team to work inside the house, dusting for prints and searching for anything unusual or out of place. Through the windows, Kaylee and the others saw them take Don's medicine into evidence.

"I wonder if someone tampered with it," Jessica said. "Do you think they can tell?"

Kaylee nodded. "They'll analyze the pills."

Wilfred groaned. "Why would someone hurt Don? I sure hope it wasn't because of our business arrangement."

Kaylee couldn't see another connection at the moment, but that didn't mean one didn't exist. "All we can do is take it step by step and see what the evidence shows us."

Nick appeared in the doorway. "A couple of things. First of all, the place has been wiped down. Very few prints anywhere, except where Mr. Heaton moved around."

"He uses a cleaning service," Kaylee said. "I saw the card on the refrigerator."

Nick frowned. "I've never seen a cleaning service that thorough. But we'll check on when they were last here. Also, does this belong to any of you?" He held up a lime-green windbreaker.

Kaylee would have recognized that particularly poisonous shade anywhere, but the flying club patch confirmed it. *Pamela's jacket.*

13

Kaylee gaped at the windbreaker. Had Pamela accompanied David out here to visit Don?

But she'd seen her in the jacket after his death at the funeral home.

"That's not mine," Jessica said, "and Kaylee wasn't wearing it."

"It's Pamela Smythe's," Kaylee said. "At least, I'm pretty sure it is. I've seen her wearing one exactly like it."

Nick studied the jacket, front and back, even checking the label. "Size small. Would that fit Pamela?"

"I think so," Kaylee said. "She's pretty short."

"We found it over the back of a chair, as if it'd been put there recently," Nick said. "Or overlooked by Don while tidying up."

Wilfred's brow knit in confusion and Kaylee sensed the wheels were turning in his mind. "Any idea why Pam would visit Don?" she asked him.

The older man shook his head. "I guess that's a question for Pamela—or Don, once he's alert again." His voice shook slightly. "I sure hope he pulls through. Don has been a good friend of mine for years."

"I hope so too." Nick put a hand on Wilfred's shoulder. "I don't have any more questions right now, if you folks want to get going."

"I'm ready whenever you are," Reese said to the others.

"Let's go then," Wilfred said. "Deputy, I sure hope you figure out what happened here."

"I hope so too, for Mr. Heaton's sake." Nick's eyes were somber. "Before you leave, can I have a word with you, Kaylee?"

"Of course." Kaylee followed Nick around to the other side of the house, out of earshot. "I found a silverpuff patch out by the airstrip," she told him. "When I get back to Orcas, I'll check and see if it's a match with the seeds you've already collected."

"That's good." Nick's tone was distant, as if he was barely listening. "I wanted to ask you—" He broke off to peer back the way they had come. "Were you with Wilfred the entire time?"

Kaylee swiftly put two and two together. "You're concerned he may have tampered with evidence."

Nick lowered his voice. "I have to ask, since he's our official suspect." He took a breath, then asked, "Whose idea was it to come out here?"

"It was Wilfred's," Kaylee admitted, not liking the direction of this conversation. But she needed to be honest. "He was worried about Don, and he wanted to find out about the loan paperwork."

"That's what he said." Nick plucked at his bottom lip, gazing off into the trees. "So, were you with Wilfred the entire time?"

Kaylee's heart sank. "No, actually. Jess and I went out to the field after we called 911. I was collecting seeds, and she went to the plane for water." Then she felt a wave of relief. "But Reese was there. Ask him."

Nick's eyebrows lifted. "The whole time you were gone?"

"I believe so." Kaylee gestured toward the other side of the house. "Want me to go get him?"

"Please," Nick said. "Then you can leave."

Kaylee sent Reese to talk to Nick, shrugging when Jessica and Wilfred gave her curious looks. To her relief, Reese and Nick's conversation was brief. Soon, they were buckled into the plane and lifting off from the grassy runway, Wilfred in command.

The air was calm as they flew back to Orcas Island, but pilots and passengers remained silent. Kaylee watched lights appear on the dark islands like delicate links in a fine gold chain. But even as she took in the gorgeous night, her mind whirred with speculation and questions.

Wilfred was Don's friend, Lorraine's company cleaned for him, and David and Pamela had both visited him. The silverpuff seeds in her tote were likely evidence of David's visit. She had no doubt they would match the ones from David's cuff and plane, not after seeing Pamela's jacket there.

Don was obviously very wealthy, judging by his home and his ability to loan Wilfred money. Had David and Pamela approached him about the development? Since Don was a pilot, that made sense. What didn't seem as logical was someone trying to hurt the older man. But Kaylee didn't believe in coincidences, and she doubted his sudden illness was one.

The plane angled for the descent into the airport, the runway lights guiding them home. Kaylee whispered a prayer that Don would pull through, that he wouldn't become another casualty.

Mary called as Jessica and Kaylee were headed toward the parking lot. "Good timing," Kaylee said. "We just landed." She could hear excited yipping in the background. "How's my boy?"

Her assistant chuckled. "He's been having a great time playing ball with Herb. But when I said I was going to call you, he dropped everything to—for lack of a better word—hound me."

Kaylee foraged for her keys. "I'll be over to get him as soon as I drop Jess off."

"Why don't you both stop by? I'll have Herb throw on some steaks when you get here."

"Steak?" Kaylee's belly rumbled. "Oh Mary, that sounds wonderful. I'm starving."

"So am I," Jessica piped. "Let me text Luke and tell him what's up." She pulled out her phone and texted while strolling around to the passenger side.

"Jess and I are both in," Kaylee told Mary. "See you soon."

"That was really fun," Jessica declared as they set off toward Mary's house. "Besides finding Don, I mean. I'll definitely have to schedule a time for Wilfred to take Luke and me up. Luke would love it."

Kaylee drove slowly along the dark roads, watching for deer and other animals that liked to come out in the evening. "I'm glad Wilfred offers scenic tours."

Jessica stared out the window at the passing countryside. "I sure hope Don is okay." She shuddered. "It's a good thing we showed up when we did."

"I agree." Kaylee settled back in the seat, trying to get comfortable. She was bone-tired, and with the Apple Fest starting tomorrow, she needed to get a good night's sleep. "Nick asked me about Wilfred, if I'd kept him in view the whole time we were there."

Jessica gasped. "I wondered what he wanted, especially after you sent Reese to see him."

"Yeah, talk about awkward. But I don't blame Nick. Wilfred is still the main suspect. But I don't think I've ever met a less devious person."

"He's a sweetheart," Jessica said. "I can see why DeeDee is so protective of him."

Kaylee signaled and slowed to turn onto Mary's street. She lived in a quiet residential area of Turtle Cove, on a lane lined with comfortable ranch homes. Mary and Herb had purchased the home as newlyweds almost four decades ago.

They pulled into the driveway and parked behind Mary's car. The front porch lights were on, welcoming them, and their hostess soon appeared behind the screen door.

"That was quick," Mary called, opening the door. Bear burst out and dashed down the steps and along the pathway toward his owner as quickly as his short legs would carry him. Behind him came Lily, Mary's sweet calico cat. The pair got along famously.

Kaylee hunkered down to greet Bear, then gave the blue-eyed Lily a chin rub. "Not much traffic tonight."

"And I'm glad of that. I can smell the steaks from here," Jessica said as she greeted the pets.

"Herb put the steaks on a few minutes ago." Mary stood back to let them enter.

With Bear leading the way, they walked down a short hall and entered the spacious combination kitchen and dining area at the back of the house. Through sliding glass doors, they could see Herb stationed at the grill on the patio. When he saw them, he waved the oversize fork he was holding.

"Have a seat," Mary said, herding them toward the table. "Iced tea? Water?"

"Water is fine, thanks," Kaylee said, sliding into a chair. Bear sat at her feet, resting his warm body against her ankles.

"I'll take the same," Jessica said as she sat across from Kaylee.

Mary grabbed a pitcher of water from the refrigerator. "Go ahead, help yourselves to salad. Herb will be in shortly."

Both potato and tossed salads were on the table, so they went ahead and loaded their plates.

After handing out waters, Mary perched on a chair and dished up her own salad. "How'd it go?"

Kaylee shook her head. "Not well, Mary. We found Don Heaton unconscious." She picked up a bottle of dressing and squeezed some onto her salad.

"No! That's awful."

The sliding door opened and Herb ferried in the perfectly cooked steaks. While they ate, Jessica and Kaylee filled the Bishops in on their visit to the island. As Mary was serving strawberry shortcake for dessert, Kaylee's phone rang. It was Wilfred.

"Don is awake," he said, his tone jubilant. "He still can't communicate well but it looks like he'll pull through."

"That's great, Wilfred." After a few more pleasantries, Kaylee hung up the phone and conveyed the news to her friends. Then, overcome with relief, she allowed her head to sag onto her hands. She could fall asleep sitting right here at Mary's table.

"Which hospital is he in?" Mary asked.

"The paramedics said they were taking him to one in Seattle," Jessica answered. "It would be better equipped to handle his case."

Mary nodded approvingly. "Good. Hopefully he's out of the woods."

Kaylee silently echoed that hope. Besides simply wanting Wilfred's friend to get well, perhaps Don would be able to shed light on the mystery of David's death—and his own illness.

Soon after, Kaylee and Jessica departed, thanking the Bishops for their last-minute hospitality.

Once in the car, Jessica said, "DeeDee is taking the first shift at the booth tomorrow. I'll be down later, after the breakfast rush."

"I'm on first shift too, while Mary opens the shop," Kaylee said. That reminded Kaylee that she needed to pick up the inventory at the store. She'd forgotten all about it. She gave a huge sigh.

"What was that for?" Jessica asked. When Kaylee explained, she said, "Let's take a detour. I'll help you load the van."

"Are you sure?" Kaylee asked. "We're almost to your place."

"What kind of friend would I be if I didn't help you? You're as done in as I am." Jessica sent Luke another text explaining what they were doing while Kaylee changed course and headed downtown.

Kaylee parked in back, where she planned to leave her SUV. First, she transferred the tote with the silverpuff seeds to the delivery van, telling herself she'd stop by the funeral chapel when she had a chance during her busy schedule the next day. *If I have a chance, that is.*

Kaylee, Jessica, and Bear entered the store through the rear door to reach the inventory, which Mary had placed in boxes stacked in the workroom. Kaylee silently blessed her assistant, who had made the job a simple matter of carrying the boxes outside to the van.

"Those two stacks are it," Kaylee said, pointing.

"Is that all? We'll have it loaded in no time," Jessica said, then grabbed the first box and headed out the door with Bear following.

Kaylee bent to pick up her own, but the sounds of Jessica's screams followed by Bear's muffled barking from inside the van made her drop it with a thud and race outside.

"What's wrong?" Kaylee called. In the dim light, she saw Jessica and Bear standing near the rear of the van, where Bear was still carrying on. "Hush, Bear."

He gave a final yelp that ended in a whine.

A dark shape moved forward to a better position under the yard light. "I'm sorry. I didn't mean to startle you."

With a shock of surprise, Kaylee recognized Brett Horne, the airport manager. It took a second, since she'd never seen him outside the Turtle Cove Airport.

Jessica put a hand to her chest. "I'm thankful I didn't drop that box of wreaths. They might not have made it." She gestured toward the box, safely inside the back of the vehicle.

With a wince, Kaylee thought about the box she'd dumped. Hopefully whatever was inside wasn't terribly fragile. She gathered her wits and asked, "How are you, Brett?" *And what are you doing here?*

"I was on a walk around the block when I realized your shop was here. I haven't lived on the island that long."

"It's a great place," Jessica said. "And your job certainly seems interesting."

"Oh, it is." He took a step toward them, shoes crunching on loose gravel. "I heard you guys rescued Don Heaton today. He's a friend of my f-father."

Now he's getting to the point. "Yes, we went to visit and discovered that he was ill," Kaylee said, "so we called for an emergency helicopter."

Brett was near the van now. "Any idea what was wrong with him?"

"I'm afraid not," Jessica said. "You'll have to check with the hospital." Her tone was brisk, and Kaylee wondered if Brett was making her uncomfortable.

Kaylee didn't like him looming there, in the dark. "Brett, I hate to be rude, but we have to load the van. Big day tomorrow."

Brett retreated. "Oh yes, that's right. The Apple Fest. Sorry, I'll let you go." His footsteps faded as he disappeared into the dark.

"That was weird," Jessica whispered once he was gone.

"It sure was," Kaylee agreed. She couldn't put her finger on anything specific, but something felt off about the encounter. Maybe it was time to dig into Brett Horne's background a little.

14

The Apple Fest opened at midmorning, so Kaylee let herself sleep in, figuring it would only take half an hour to set up the display. She carried a mug of coffee outside and wandered around the garden with Bear for a while. She liked to spend time among the flowers, enjoying their scents and beauty. Even now, in the fall, a number of perennials were still blooming, and the container annuals were valiantly producing.

She was relaxing in an Adirondack chair and thinking about refilling her cup when her cell phone dinged with a text. She pulled the phone out of her robe pocket and checked the display.

The message was from DeeDee. *Emergency at the farm. Wilfred in deep trouble with inspector. Please come.*

Kaylee frowned, suddenly concerned for poor Wilfred. Which inspector was DeeDee talking about? And deep trouble? That sounded ominous. She texted DeeDee saying she'd meet her in half an hour.

"Come on, Bear," she said as she stood up. "Let's get going."

At her words, the dog turned from the bush he was nosing around and trotted across the grass, tail wagging.

Kaylee showered and dressed, packed breakfast to go, and grabbed Bear's leash. Then she hopped in the van and set out for the farm. On the bright side, it was next door to her ultimate destination.

At the apple orchard, she let Bear into the farmhouse since animals weren't allowed in the packing shed, then went to the shed to find out what had DeeDee so upset.

"Thanks so much for coming, Kaylee," DeeDee called from

where she stood with Reese and Jessica.

"What's going on?" Kaylee asked. She noticed Wilfred and Lorraine talking to a slight, bald man wearing glasses and holding a clipboard. They were examining bins of apples stacked on a forklift.

"That's the organic inspector," DeeDee said, indicating the stranger. "Someone phoned in a tip that Wilfred's apples aren't organic. That guy's here to go through everything with a fine-tooth comb."

Kaylee's brow furrowed in confusion. "I don't get it. Wilfred doesn't use chemicals to grow them, right? How could the apples suddenly not be organic?" Her thoughts briefly landed on the rat poison found in the shed, but she didn't believe for a second that the package had come in contact with any of the trees or fruit on the farm.

The inspector held up an apple and examined it, then handed it to Wilfred. Kaylee could tell something was wrong from the farmer's body language. He handed it to Lorraine, who yelped, "How did that get there?"

"Let's find out what's going on," Kaylee said. The four of them strode across the concrete floor.

"I'm telling you, that's not my apple," Wilfred said. "It's a Fuji." He took a big bite out of it. "Yep. A good one too. Problem is, I don't grow Fuji apples."

Kaylee peered at the apple in Wilfred's hand and noticed a sticker on it. Seeing her curiosity, the inspector said in a droning voice, "The code on a produce sticker shows how a piece of produce was grown. If there are only four digits, it was conventionally grown, like this Fuji. If there is a nine before the four digits, that indicates the produce is organic. You can't have both in the same bin."

"You mean the organic apples are now contaminated?" Kaylee asked. The assumption seemed far-fetched, but she supposed some pesticide might rub off onto the organic apples.

The inspector nodded.

"So what does this mean?" DeeDee asked. "Are the apples ruined?"

"No, not ruined," the inspector said, "but they can't be sold as organic." His tight-lipped smile held a touch of smug satisfaction. "You'll have to label them all as conventional."

A thin shriek burst from Lorraine, resembling the piercing whistle of a teakettle. "This is outrageous." She stamped a small, sneakered foot. "Someone broke in here and planted those apples. We did not mix organic and conventional fruit."

The inspector's brows rose. "Madam, I have never heard of such a thing. Who would do that?" He tutted in disbelief. "In any case, it's too late. The milk is spilled, the horse is stolen, the sky has fallen, and so forth." A smirk flitted across his face at this recitation of farm-related idioms.

Wilfred's shoulders sagged in resignation. "All right, then. I'll find some stickers—I can call another orchard—and we'll get to work." Setting his tired eyes on the inspector, he asked, "Is there anything else today?"

The man checked his clipboard, then shook his head with seeming disappointment. "No, you're all set for now. But you'd better scour this building before you bring in any more apples. If you want to sell them as organic, that is."

Lorraine pushed up her sleeves. "Don't worry about that, young man. We're expert cleaners around here."

"Hope so." The inspector clicked his pen closed and tucked it into his shirt pocket. "Give me a call when you're done and I'll be back to inspect the premises. Good day." He nodded, then bolted toward the exit, apparently eager to be gone.

Once he was safely in his vehicle and driving away, Lorraine and DeeDee broke into protests and exclamations. As for Wilfred, he stared out the open back door at the rows of trees laden with fruit.

Kaylee guessed that he was worried about the delay in the harvest. "We'll help you as much as we can, Wilfred."

"That's right," Reese said. "I'll get the band to come help clean this evening before rehearsal."

"You mean the Appleseeds?" Jessica's eyes twinkled. "I'm sure Luke will agree."

"I'd appreciate it, Reese," Wilfred said. "And if you need rehearsal space, the least I can do is offer my house for your practice. I'll have a meal brought in for everyone too." He pulled his phone from the pocket of his baggy pants. "But first, I'd better get those labels over here right away."

The owner of a nearby orchard drove over with a box of labels right away, eager to help a fellow farmer. After he left, the group got to work, peeling off organic stickers and replacing them with those for conventionally grown fruit. The change meant a significant price decrease for Wilfred, since organic went for more money. However, these apples were destined for direct sales at the Apple Fest, not to a wholesale account, so Wilfred felt he could absorb the cost.

They found six Fuji apples scattered among a dozen forty-pound crates, even though only one would have been enough to overturn the apple cart, so to speak.

Wilfred was about to tip the rogue apples into the trash when Kaylee stopped him. "You really should bag up one or two. They're evidence that someone broke in here."

"Good point." His smile was sad. "I just wanted to get rid of them."

"Understandable." Kaylee glanced around. "Do you have any plastic zipper storage bags? One of those would do."

"In the break room." Wilfred started for a small room off the main packing area, but Kaylee held up a hand.

"I'll get it." She gestured toward Reese, who was climbing up onto the seat of a forklift. "You stay here and supervise. I don't know if he's ever driven one of those things before."

Kaylee quickly found a box of gallon-size bags in a drawer. She retrieved a bag and carried it out to the main room. Two Fuji apples were sitting on a table so she slid them into the bag, then used a marker to write a notation and date. The chances of tracing them back to a purchase were practically nil, since they were common in grocery stores, but she had to try. Plus they were proof of the crime—perishable perhaps, but evidence all the same.

Reese maneuvered the forklift toward the garage door opening. Wilfred's truck was waiting outside with its ramp down for loading.

Jessica and DeeDee stripped off plastic gloves as they walked toward Kaylee. "I've got to get back to the bakery," Jessica said.

"Would you mind following me over to the airport so I can drop off the van and then driving me to pick up my car?" Kaylee asked. "I'm going to leave The Flower Patch van here until the end of the Apple Fest. We can put the inventory inside overnight."

DeeDee's eyes widened. "I didn't even think of that. Some people have more secure booths than ours."

"Yeah, usually we're inside a building at these things," Jessica said. "Of course no one wants to steal stale baked goods, so I've never had that problem."

"I doubt any of your goodies will be left at the end of the day, so no worries there," Kaylee said.

Jessica laughed. "I appreciate the vote of confidence. Ready to go?"

"Sure," Kaylee said. "DeeDee, I'll see you at the booth in a little while."

Wilfred hurried toward them. "DeeDee, do you think you can go visit Don for me today?"

DeeDee glanced at her friends. "The best laid plans, right?" She turned to her godfather. "Shouldn't you go, Wilfred? I'm sure he wants to see you."

"I can't go." Wilfred sighed heavily. "I can't leave San Juan County under the terms of my bail. And he's in Seattle."

"Hold on a minute," DeeDee said. "We'll figure it out."

"One problem is our jam-packed schedule today," Kaylee explained. "We've got the booth, our businesses, and helping clean here later. Going to Seattle and back takes hours." She voiced these reasonable objections with regret. She would love to talk to Don and see what light he could shed on what had happened to him—and perhaps on David's death too.

Wilfred smiled. "I have a solution. How do you feel about a seaplane ride?"

After putting in a morning shift at the Apple Fest booth, which did brisk business, and afternoon hours at their respective shops, DeeDee joined Kaylee at The Flower Patch for the drive to Eastsound to meet Wilfred's pilot friend Tuck.

"I feel a little guilty about not helping clean at the farm," Kaylee said as she slid her SUV into one of many vacant parking spaces at the marina. This time of day, the waterfront was fairly quiet.

"So do I," DeeDee said, "but seeing Don is important too." She gathered her raincoat and handbag. "He might know something that will help clear Wilfred."

"I sure hope so." Kaylee reached into the back seat for the cheerful floral arrangement she'd made for Don. "It'd be nice to make some real progress on this case." Every time they seemed to be getting somewhere, another piece of confusing evidence popped up. *Like Pamela's windbreaker,* she thought as she grabbed her own turquoise jacket, a much less jarring shade than the widow's.

They set off across the parking lot, the seaplanes clearly visible at one end of the dock area. The colorful aircraft rose and fell in the gentle tide, secured like boats at moorings or alongside a dock. A man waited beside a yellow one, contemplating the harbor scene.

"That must be Tuck," DeeDee said.

Short and muscular, with a wide-legged stance, the pilot gave an impression of seasoned strength. His tanned, weather-beaten face and white hair reinforced that image. He thrust out a hand with a grin. "DeeDee Wilcox? Kaylee Bleu? Welcome aboard."

He helped them climb inside with their belongings, a maneuver that involved stepping on the wide floats and a bit of scrambling. They both sat in the back, at Tuck's suggestion. "Relax and enjoy the ride," he said before climbing into the pilot's seat.

Taxiing and taking off in the seaplane was similar to the Cherokee, but they skimmed across the water instead of racing down the runway. Soon they were up in the air and curving around the island before heading toward the city. Kaylee spotted the ferry below, which from this height appeared to be only crawling. They were literally saving hours by traveling this way.

As in Wilfred's plane, they wore headsets, which kept the noise down and allowed them to talk to each other. Now and then, Tuck pointed out something of interest, including a pod of whales. Although the day was shading toward evening, the animals' massive shapes were visible in the lighter water.

Clouds thickened near the mainland so Tuck flew above them. Kaylee and DeeDee gasped and murmured at the beauty of the setting sun gilding the fluffy formations. After what seemed too short a time, they descended back through the cover and emerged above Lake Union, their destination. The jumbled gray shapes of downtown surrounded the freshwater lake, including the distinctive Space Needle. In the background, Mount Rainier kept watch over the city, clouds fringing the peak like a collar.

The plane descended toward the water and touched down, then glided to the docks, the water rushing past the floats. Tuck cut the engine, and they drifted neatly into his selected berth. He turned in his seat. "Welcome to Seattle, ladies. I'll be waiting here for you when you get back from the hospital." He made a salute. "Give Don my best."

After he helped them onto the dock, they made their way through the wharf area to the street. There they called a cab to take them to the hospital. Seattle was as busy and vibrant as Kaylee remembered, but as she watched the passing scene through the cab window, she saw it with fresh eyes, like a visitor. The transformation from an old life teaching in the city to living on the island was complete, she realized.

Turtle Cove was home now. And she certainly didn't miss the traffic noise, concrete and pavement everywhere, or the need to always be on guard for unwanted encounters.

Like when a man jostled her as she and DeeDee crossed a side street to the hospital entrance. Kaylee stumbled and almost dropped the flower arrangement.

"Are you okay?" DeeDee asked, steadying the bouquet. She glanced at the cars speeding by, driving too fast in the narrow lane. "Come on. Let's go."

Safely on the sidewalk, Kaylee glanced back at the man, who was striding away as if nothing had happened. Something about him seemed familiar, but his ball cap and bulky jacket prevented her from getting a good look at his face.

Once she and DeeDee reached the entrance, the double door hissing open, she said, "Did you recognize the man who bumped into me?"

DeeDee frowned. "Recognize him? No, I was too busy helping you save the flowers."

Kaylee stepped aside to let an attendant push a wheelchair past them. "I thought maybe he was someone we know. But I must have imagined it." She was probably on edge, seeing bad guys everywhere. And who could blame her? Don's incident might well be attempted murder.

"Wilfred told me Don is in room 306," DeeDee explained as they crossed the gleaming tile floor toward the elevator. A few minutes later, they had followed signs down a couple of corridors and found their destination.

Don opened one eye as they entered the hospital room. "You caught me. I was napping." He chuckled, then his brow knit in confusion. "If you're here for the other guy, he went home." A second bed was empty, stripped of covers.

"No, we're here to see you," DeeDee said. "I'm Wilfred's goddaughter, DeeDee Wilcox. And this is my friend, Kaylee Bleu. She found you at your house when you were sick."

Don pushed himself to a more upright position. "If Wilfred sent you, then I know you're good folks. Thanks for coming to visit an old man."

DeeDee bustled to the bed to assist him. "We're glad to be here."

"Nice to meet you, Don." Kaylee set the arrangement on the wide windowsill and started tweaking flowers. "I hope you're feeling better."

After sitting up with DeeDee's help, he reached for a tall paper cup on the bedside table. "Getting there. They said they'd spring me tomorrow." He brought the straw close to his lips. "Did you bring me this? Looks like a mint shake—my favorite."

DeeDee shook her head. "No, it wasn't us."

An instinct made Kaylee leap toward the bed, arms outstretched. "Don't drink that! It might be poisoned."

15

Don paused, the straw still near his mouth. "What do you mean, poisoned?"

DeeDee gently took the cup from his fingers and set it on the tray. "David was poisoned, remember? Kaylee is being extra cautious."

"I may be overreacting, but better safe than sorry." Kaylee used a tissue to whisk the cup away. "Did they find out what happened to you, Don?"

Although a big man, he suddenly appeared frail. "They said there was some kind of mix-up with my medication. The doctor thinks I took the wrong dosage."

Kaylee wondered if the sheriff's department had gotten lab results back yet—and what Nick thought about them.

"I doubt that," DeeDee said crisply. "Have you ever done that before?"

Don shook his head. "No, I put out the day's pills each morning. But I do have a couple of new ones, so maybe I got confused."

A nurse bustled into the room. "Time to take your vitals, Mr. Heaton." Something about the three of them must have struck her as strange because she asked, "Is everything okay in here?"

Kaylee held up the milkshake. "Did you see who left this here?"

She shook her head. "I'm sorry. Is there a problem with it?" She turned to Don. "You're not allergic to milk products, are you?"

"No ma'am. Just wondering." Don adjusted his position and held out his arm to have his blood pressure taken.

Kaylee's gaze met DeeDee's, and she tipped her head toward

the hall. "We're going to step out for a second, Don. We'll be back." To keep it safe from being tossed out, Kaylee carried the milkshake with her.

"You really think it might be poisoned?" DeeDee eyed the drink as if it had fangs.

"Maybe." Kaylee shrugged. "After David's death and the problem with Don's medications, I think we need to be really cautious."

DeeDee sucked in a breath. "You don't think it was the man who bumped into you, do you?"

Kaylee wondered, in the back of her mind, about that very thing. But she said, "I don't want to make assumptions. Let's ask Don if anyone else was here today." The cup was still cold, so it hadn't been sitting out long. The idea of calling the local police floated through her mind. But what would she tell them? They weren't likely to spend money on lab tests without any evidence of a crime. Her suspicions weren't enough.

The nurse exited the room. "He's all yours." She halted. "It gets pretty hectic around here during visiting hours. I'm sorry we can't tell you who was here earlier."

"That's okay," DeeDee said. "I didn't want Don to have too much sugar before bed, that's all. But he never listens to me."

"I hear you." The nurse laughed. "He's not on a restricted diet, but I really have to watch the ones who are. Relatives smuggle forbidden treats in all the time."

Kaylee could imagine. "Thanks for taking such good care of him."

The nurse smiled at her and strode away, her shoes squeaking on the tile.

The two women went back inside Don's room, Kaylee still carrying the milkshake. She would give Nick a call, she decided, and see what he had to say about how she should proceed. Not for the first time, she was glad that she had the authority to collect evidence for the sheriff's department.

"The only person here today was Pamela Smythe." Don rolled his eyes. "That woman yatters so much, I fell asleep while she was talking."

Kaylee remembered the jacket but didn't mention it yet. "You know Pamela?" Maybe Pamela had left the milkshake once Don was asleep.

Don plucked at the sheet, newly tucked and straightened. "I've known her for years. Her and David both. We were part of the same flying club here on the mainland. I bought my island about five years ago, and about a year later, they moved to Orcas."

"What about Brett Horne's father?" Kaylee asked, her nerves tingling. Maybe all these pilots were tied together somehow. "Was he part of the group?"

"Oh yes, Lon certainly was." His brows drew together and his lips flattened into a fine line. "Another one gone too soon."

Kaylee's chest tightened in dread at this news. But before she could speak, DeeDee asked, "What happened?"

Don lifted a big, freckled hand, then let it drop. "He ran a charter service for decades, flying people and packages all over the islands. Then the FAA found some issues and . . . well, his business went under. Once you lose trust as a pilot, you're sunk." He stared down at the sheets, and his voice was so low the women had to strain to hear him. "The poor man killed himself. It wasn't so much the bankruptcy as the loss of his reputation. And his flying certificate, of course."

For a commercial pilot, a certificate was critical, Kaylee had gathered. Kind of like a truck driver losing his license.

"Something wasn't right about that," Don muttered. "Never could wrap my head around it. Lon was too conscientious and detail-minded to let things slip the way they said he did."

Again, Kaylee's nerves tingled. She wondered if there was

more to the story than Don knew. Was David somehow involved with Lon's downfall? Lorraine had said something about conflict between the two men. But even if not, maybe Brett *thought* he had been. She contemplated asking for more details, but Don was clearly tired, so she didn't press. She'd see what she could find out through research.

DeeDee must have noticed the patient's exhaustion as well because she said, "We'll get going soon, Don. But before we do, can you tell us anything that happened the day you got sick?"

After a moment Don shrugged. "Not much. I didn't see anyone all day. The day before, Pamela came out to visit, along with Lon's son, Brett." A sly smile crossed his face. "That time I managed to stay awake. Maybe because he was there. He didn't let her talk my ear off."

That was confirmation of how the jacket got there. Kaylee thought of the silverpuff seeds. "How about David? Did he visit you too?"

Don snorted. "Oh yeah. He tried to get me to invest in his development scheme at the airport. I told him I didn't need a fly-in home since I already have one."

"I heard they sell for a lot," Kaylee said. "Might be a good investment."

"True." Don frowned, his eyes dark. "The last time he came, he finally talked me into a financial transaction. For a while, he'd been trying to buy the loan I gave Wilfred. I finally gave in, because I need the cash. All my money is tied up in investments."

"You can sell a loan?" DeeDee asked.

Don nodded. "Yes. Banks do it all the time with mortgages. Then the new owner collects the debt."

That's what David had been talking about with Wilfred at the vendor meeting, Kaylee realized. He wanted to buy the loan so he could try to force Wilfred off his land.

Don sniffed, his nose twitching slightly. "What a mistake that was, selling the loan. I never should have done it. To be honest, I was avoiding Wilfred's calls yesterday morning before I passed out because I thought he'd found out about it. And then he goes and saves my life." He sniffed again. "He didn't deserve for me to put him in debt with a guy like David Smythe."

DeeDee's face paled, and Kaylee could guess why. Don's statement strengthened the case against Wilfred, implicating him as David's killer.

After they left Don's room, Kaylee found a quiet spot to call Nick.

"Are you going to tell him what Don said about the loan?" DeeDee asked, her face twisted with anxiety.

Kaylee perched on a too-hard plastic chair in a small, empty waiting room. "I have to. It looks worse if we hide things." She found her phone in a side pocket of her tote. "But Wilfred certainly didn't leave the milkshake here. If they find something . . ." Her words trailed off as she dialed.

"I'm going to the cafeteria for coffee. Want one?" At Kaylee's nod, DeeDee gave a wave and disappeared down the corridor.

Nick's phone rang a few times before he picked up. "Kaylee. Where are you?"

"In Seattle, visiting Don Heaton. Why? Did you need me?"

"Not exactly. I went by the Bates farm a little while ago and didn't see you."

Kaylee glanced at the wall clock. The gang must have been cleaning the packing shed when he was there. "Something new I should know about?"

"No, just telling Wilfred that Don Heaton was awake." Keys clacked in the background. "I wanted to see his reaction."

"He found that out this morning. I could have told you his reaction," Kaylee said with a snort. "Excited and happy. That's why DeeDee and I flew over this evening: Wilfred wanted us to check on his friend, since he can't leave the islands." She swallowed hard, knowing that she had to tell Nick what she had heard. But first she'd mention the milkshake. "The strangest thing happened and I need your advice."

"Go ahead."

She explained about the milkshake, then said, "Don told us Pamela Smythe came to see him today." She let Nick absorb this, then added, "The nurse didn't see who left it, and Don didn't know either. I'd like to have it tested. I know I might be overreacting, but I don't think we should take any chances."

"I agree. Take it into evidence and we'll have the lab run it. They're still checking Don's medication to see if there was any tampering."

Kaylee's chest tightened. It was time. "There's more."

"What's that?"

"Don told us that David did visit him. Don needed cash, and David bought a loan Don gave Wilfred. Remember the paperwork that was missing from Wilfred's office?"

Nick was nothing if not sharp, and he put the pieces together immediately. "So David had leverage over Wilfred and his property."

"I'm afraid so." Kaylee slumped back in the uncomfortable chair. They still didn't know anything definitive. Fingers were still pointing in all directions.

"Thanks for calling, Kaylee." By the warmth in his voice, she could tell that he really appreciated her help. "And for being so honest. Are you two heading back tonight?"

DeeDee appeared in the doorway and handed Kaylee a

welcome to-go cup of coffee. "We are," Kaylee told the deputy. "We both have to put in time at the Apple Fest tomorrow as well as our shops."

At her friend's gesture indicating they should get going, Kaylee stood, still holding the phone. "In fact, we're leaving now. See you soon, Nick."

It was well after dark when they landed in Eastsound, the seaplane skimming across inky water to the dock. Kaylee longed to head for Wildflower Cottage and bed, but first she had to pick up Bear at the apple orchard. Mary had offered to take him for the evening, and rather than leave him alone at home, Kaylee had readily agreed on his behalf.

Kaylee and DeeDee's first stop was the sheriff's department, where Kaylee handed over the milkshake, which she had packed in a cup of ice from the hospital cafeteria. Then they drove out to the fruit farm, where a lively rock melody greeted them. The Appleseeds had set up inside a large shed, which was open to the night air. As Kaylee and DeeDee walked across the grass toward the building, Polly and Zoe came dancing to meet them. Bear trotted out behind them, tail wagging when he spotted his owner.

"Mommy!" Polly cried. "We wondered when you'd get here."

Kaylee bent over and scooped Bear into her arms, a maneuver he rewarded with a lick across the face. She laughed.

"What are you doing here, girls?" DeeDee asked. "Isn't it a school night?" Although her husband was rehearsing, he would normally get a babysitter.

"Not tonight, Mom," Zoe said. "It's a teacher's workshop tomorrow."

DeeDee gasped, her expression harried. "Oh no. I forgot all about that. I don't have childcare lined up."

"They can come to the booth with me," Kaylee said. "Do you want to help me sell things at the Apple Fest, girls?"

Zoe and Polly jumped up and down, shrieking with delight. "We'd love to," Zoe said. "I'm really good at counting money."

"So am I," Polly said. Her big eyes were pleading. She clasped her hands, begging. "Please, Mommy?"

"All right," DeeDee said. "But promise you'll be good for Kaylee, Mary, and Jessica in the morning. You have to listen to what they say." To Kaylee, she said, "I'll be there all afternoon."

"We promise, Mom," Zoe said, slipping an arm through her mother's. "Now come listen to Dad's band."

They strolled as a group to the shed, where the band played a few more numbers. Kaylee was impressed at how much better they were than the first time. They seemed to have found a groove.

"How'd we do?" Reese asked Kaylee after the practice ended.

"You sounded great," she said with sincerity. She stood and watched as he dismantled his drum kit and packed it into a case. With their simpler instruments, the other musicians left first with their families, a chorus of "good night" filling the air.

Wilfred came over from the house and puttered around the shed, making sure all was in order. When he spotted Kaylee, he hurried over to her. "How was Don?"

"He's doing well," Kaylee said. She hesitated, not wanting to upset Wilfred by mentioning the milkshake and a possible poisoning attempt. That could wait until the results came back, she decided. But he needed to know what had happened with his debt to Don. "He did tell me something important about David, though."

Reese paused in the act of coiling an amplifier cord.

Wilfred's gaze sharpened and his hands fisted at his sides. "Something to clear my name, I hope." Wilfred's voice was hoarse.

Kaylee's heart sank. There was no easy way to word it, so she said the minimum. "David bought your loan from Don."

With a groan, Wilfred rubbed a hand over his face. "I can't

believe Don would do that to me. He knew David wanted to buy my land."

"Some friend," Reese muttered, shaking his head.

"I don't think he considered that angle when it happened. He was short on cash. From what he said, I think he regrets it." Kaylee winced in sympathy for Wilfred, knowing that a friend's betrayal cut deep. An idea dawned in her mind. *Maybe David forced him to do it—but how?* "And there might have been extenuating circumstances."

"I sure hope so," Wilfred said. His expression and voice were bleak. "Otherwise I've lost a friend."

Reese latched the drum case cover. "I'm all set here. I just need to carry these to the truck."

Wilfred shook off his gloom, good humor returning to his features. "What do you think about doing some aerobatic flying, Reese? I'll be taking up a 1939 Waco E series biplane in the vintage plane exhibition tomorrow. They're expecting quite a crowd for the show."

Reese whistled in delight. "Are you kidding? I'd love to. Where'd you get the Waco E? I read they only made those for a few years, which is a shame."

"Brett Horne called tonight and asked me to take her up. He said he's come down with a bug or something, so he can't do it."

Kaylee experienced a twinge of concern. Then she shrugged it off. *Not every stomach pain or pang indicates poisoning . . . right?*

16

The next morning at the airport, Brett seemed okay, although he was walking around holding a bottle of liquid antacid. "Please take care of my baby," he said to Wilfred and Reese, who were doing a preflight inspection. "My pop left it to me. My inheritance, you might say."

Polly and Zoe were watching the proceedings with Kaylee, who hadn't opened the booth yet. When she'd seen the men inspecting the sleek yellow biplane, she and the girls had wandered over.

"Is Reese going up in that airplane?" Polly asked, her eyes wide with amazement.

"He sure is," Zoe said. "And he's doing tricks."

"Tricks?" Polly's voice rose to a squeak. "Like a dog?"

Wilfred chuckled. "Sort of. We roll, dive, and spin. It's great fun."

Reese went a little green at this description, Kaylee noticed, but he continued checking items off the list. He brightened a bit when Wilfred added, "And we wear parachutes, just in case."

Brett took a swig of chalky liquid. "Don't say that, Wilfred. I'm counting on you to bring her down safely." Another swig. "I spent the last year going over this plane prop to tail. Total reno."

Wilfred patted him on the back. "Don't worry about it, Brett. I've done all right so far. Perfect record." He smiled at the girls. "I'll be looking to make sure you're watching, okay? Cheer us on like this." He clasped his hands and waved them in the air. "Go on, you try it."

The girls complied, giggling as they did.

It was time to open the booth, so Kaylee wished the pilots

luck and steered the sisters back to their tent. On the way, they passed the concessions tent, which was already buzzing with activity. "Can we have hot chocolate?" Zoe asked. "Pretty please?"

Kaylee could use another cup of coffee herself, so she stopped to buy the hot drinks. She also let the girls pick out cookies, figuring that way the baked goods at the booth would be safe. Or at least she hoped so, but she wouldn't count on it since Jessica was bringing trays of apple tarts, mini pies, and turnovers, as well as some chocolate goodies.

The girls helped Kaylee set up The Flower Patch display, setting out the items from the van. Kaylee made a list of what had sold the day before and needed to be replaced, which Mary would deliver later. The apple wreaths had been big sellers, as expected, as had potted mums.

While Kaylee and the girls worked, throngs of spectators arrived, unfolding chairs along the runway or gathering on a set of metal bleachers. A couple of television cameras were set up to capture the action, and reporters with handheld video cameras made the circuit of the booths.

"I like these tiny apples," Polly said, her fingers lightly touching one of the wreath decorations. "They'd be so cute all over a little fake tree."

"Oh, I want one too," Zoe said. "We can put them in our rooms, on our desks where we do homework."

Polly nodded, making her ponytail bounce. "Good idea. Apples always make me think of school."

Another design to create. "That does sound cute," Kaylee said. "I'll check with Mary about supplies."

Jets roared overhead, and Kaylee glanced up to see a fighter plane racing past, followed by three others. The sound raised goose bumps on her arms.

"Wow," Polly said, her mouth hanging open.

"Exactly," Zoe agreed.

Like the other people on the field, they stopped what they were doing to watch as the planes went through fancy maneuvers. Then the four jets sped off in different directions.

Jessica pulled up in her SUV and parked beside the booth. As she hopped out, she said, "That was amazing. I'm so glad I got to see it." She opened the rear and pulled out a tray of baked goods.

Brett's voice crackled over a loudspeaker. "What a treat, ladies and gentlemen. An unexpected visit from the armed forces fighter jets." The spectators broke into applause and cheers even though the jets were long gone. "Next up, we have powered parachutes."

"One extreme to another," Jessica said. She picked up an apple tart and handed it to Polly, then gave another to Zoe. "I can see you girls are working hard."

"We are," Polly said, her mouth full.

"This is even better than the cookies Kaylee bought us," Zoe added.

Jessica shot Kaylee a teasing glance, and Kaylee smiled and shrugged her shoulders. "I like to spoil the help," Kaylee said. "They've earned it."

The brightly colored parachutes, with seats barely big enough for the pilots, buzzed through the air and then landed. *They're like flying go-carts,* Kaylee thought with amusement.

"How old do you have to be to go up in one of those?" Polly asked, a hopeful tinge in her voice.

"Older than you, I'm pretty sure," Kaylee said. She grinned at Jessica. "I think we'd better warn DeeDee that she's got a budding pilot on her hands."

Accompanied by announcements over the loudspeaker, the friends waited on shoppers, keeping an eye on the sky as various types of aircraft took off, flew overhead, and landed. The girls bagged purchases and counted change, although most shoppers used credit or debit cards. The baked goods went fast, helped by the stylish sandwich board Jessica had put up. The fact that she'd used local apples seemed to be a plus, and across the way, Wilfred's farm stand was also doing well. He'd hired a pair of teenagers to work the booth, and they were constantly busy with customers buying fruit.

"I'd like one of those turnovers, please," a man said.

Kaylee glanced up when she heard the familiar voice. Jocko McGee gave her his mischievous grin. Thankfully DeeDee wasn't here, and neither was Wilfred. "Good morning, Jocko. Enjoying the show?"

The young man munched on the turnover, his gaze on the sky where experimental aircraft were flying in formation. "Sure am." He shook his hair out of his eyes. "Have you seen Wilfred Bates around? I heard Don Heaton pulled through."

Brett's yellow biplane was lined up on the runway, waiting for the signal to take off. "Wilfred's in that Waco E," Kaylee said. "I guess you'll have to wait until he lands." She didn't offer up the fact that she'd seen Don the day before.

She didn't need to. He crammed the rest of the turnover into his mouth and chewed while pulling a tablet from his satchel. "I understand you and Mrs. Wilcox flew to Seattle last night to visit Mr. Heaton. Any comment about that?"

"None," Kaylee said, injecting a brisk tone into her voice. Jocko must have contacts on the mainland who were keeping him informed. Or at least someone who liked to talk to reporters.

Her reply didn't have the withering effect she'd hoped. Jocko turned his smile on Jessica. "How about you, Mrs. Roberts? I understand you were there when Mr. Heaton was found, collapsed in his own house."

Jessica sent Jocko an irritated glare, cutting her gaze toward the girls, who were fortunately occupied with Bear. "I don't have any comment either."

"Was Mr. Bates disappointed when he got the news about Mr. Heaton's recovery?"

Kaylee bit back a sharp retort. If this was the angle Jocko was taking, she'd warn Wilfred not to talk to him. Of course she'd have given him that advice anyway. "You can ask questions all day, but we won't have anything to say about Wilfred or Don."

Undeterred, the reporter played with his tablet for a moment, then asked, "Were you aware that Pamela Smythe is taking the helm of her late husband's development project? There's another planning board meeting about it next week."

Kaylee wasn't surprised. Despite grief over David, Pamela had to think about her future. "Sorry, Jocko. Again, no comment." She held up an apple wreath. "Can I interest you in one of these? Maybe your mom would like it."

Jessica held up another item, a birdhouse decorated with apple stencils and faux flowers. "How about this? Isn't it darling?"

As Kaylee had hoped, the sales pitches discouraged further questioning. Jocko sighed and tucked his tablet into his bag. "Thanks, but I've got to get going. Let me know if you decide you do have a comment about something."

Kaylee watched him disappear into the crowd. "I'm glad to see the last of him, that's for sure."

"He's just trying to break a big story and make his career," Jessica said. Wearing gloves, she rearranged the remaining pastries on the platters to make the display more attractive.

Polly appeared at Jessica's elbow. "Can Zoe and I go refill our water bottles inside, Mrs. Roberts?"

"It's pretty crowded. Why don't I go with you?" Jessica glanced at Kaylee. "Is that okay with you?"

"Of course," Kaylee said. "I'm fine here alone for a few."

After they left, Kaylee noticed a man standing on the fringe of the booth area, her eye caught by the sun hitting his sunglasses. Tall and slender with graying hair, he stood casually, hands in his pockets. Something about him struck her as familiar, but she couldn't put a finger on why. Maybe she'd seen him around the island or even in the shop.

Then he moved forward, looking both ways as he crossed a lane of foot traffic, and came right toward the booth. As he approached, he raised the sunglasses to his hair and squinted blue eyes at Kaylee. "Ms. Bleu? I'm Kip Bates." His voice sounded similar to Wilfred's, but it, as well as his entire appearance, had a polish the farmer lacked.

The difference between a country Bates and a city Bates. "Yes, I'm Kaylee. I'm glad to meet you, Kip."

"Same here." Still squinting, he peered around at the people, the sky, the airplanes, and the other booths. "I missed this place more than I realized." He paused when his gaze caught the sign in front of Wilfred's farm stand. "What's with the 'locally grown'? I thought we were organic."

Kaylee noted the use of "we," and smiled. Then, in case he thought she was happy about the situation, she straightened her features. "Wilfred had a little trouble with the inspector." She filled him in on what had happened.

Kip frowned. "Commercial apples in the bins? Do you think someone sabotaged him?"

"I do," Kaylee said. "He's under a lot of pressure to sell the farm." She waved a hand toward where the proposed housing development was located. "People want to build a fly-in community here and they need his land."

"Big bucks in those. I've done the books for one." A crease appeared between Kip's brows, a near mirror of Wilfred's same expression.

"So I gather," Kaylee said. "I don't disagree with the idea

in principle, but we need farms too." She hesitated, wondering how much to disclose to Kip about his father's disagreement with David Smythe. Better leave it for Wilfred, she decided.

But Kip surprised Kaylee by saying, "I take it Smythe had something to do with the development and that's why they're accusing my dad of killing him?"

"David was one of the leads on it," Kaylee admitted. "I gather he owns land, as does the airport, but they wanted to be able to build more houses."

"More houses, more money. One or two million each, I bet."

"At least." She spotted the girls and Jessica coming back across the tarmac, both girls skipping. "I'm really glad you're here, Kip. When your dad comes back, he'll be thrilled to see you, I'm sure."

"I hope so." Still holding his sunglasses, Kip swiveled around, searching the crowd. "Where is he? After I didn't find him at the farm, I checked his hangar. But he wasn't there and the plane was."

"He's flying that yellow Waco E." Kaylee pointed to the biplane, which was now taxiing down the runway. "He and Reese—a friend of mine—are going up to do a few tricks."

Kip laughed, a deep-throated, attractive bellow. "Sounds like Dad."

"Mr. Holt is taking off," Polly called as she trotted toward Kaylee. "Watch." She pointed to the plane now lifting gracefully from the runway.

"Next up is one of our top pilots, Wilfred Bates," Brett said over the loudspeaker. "He's flying my prize Waco E, folks, a gorgeous plane I spent over a year restoring." He chuckled. "Let's hope he brings her down in one piece."

Kaylee found herself crossing her fingers and released them with a laugh at her own foolishness. Wilfred was an expert pilot, and he could handle a few rolls and spins with no trouble.

Jessica returned to the booth, and Kip turned to greet her. "Hi, I'm Kip Bates."

"Kip?" Jessica's voice rose almost into a squeal. She clapped a hand over her mouth in a visible effort to calm herself. "Sorry. We were hoping to meet you."

Kaylee was grateful Jessica didn't mention how they searched high and low for the man. The less said about the Petal Pushers taking matters into their own hands, the better. "Kip, this is my good friend, Jessica Roberts. She made these scrumptious desserts with apples from your farm."

Kip inclined his head in greeting. "Nice to meet you. I'll take a mini apple pie, please. I've really missed pies made with our apples."

Kaylee put her arms around both girls and nudged them forward. "And our helpers are Polly and Zoe, DeeDee's daughters. Girls, this is Wilfred's son, Kip."

"Nice to meet you both." Kip's eyes were kind as he shook their hands, offered with solemn greetings. He paid for his treat, then stood to watch with them as Wilfred and Reese did their first trick—a barrel roll, as reported by Brett.

The crowd gasped and cheered. Queasy, Kaylee put a hand to her midriff. She could not imagine doing that in a plane.

Wilfred flew straight up, higher and higher, then forced the plane into a dive, screaming toward earth. He expertly leveled off in the nick of time and did a circle around the airport, waggling the wings in greeting.

"I'd hate to be Reese right now," Jessica whispered. "I wonder how he's holding up."

"I wonder if he'll quit his flying lessons," Kaylee joked. But she doubted it. Reese had nerves of steel.

The pair did several more tricks, then to Kaylee's relief, the plane headed back to the runway. Kaylee let out the breath she hadn't realized she was holding. They were landing at last, safe and sound.

"I'm going to head over," Kip said. "Thanks again, ladies. I hope to see you a little later."

"We'll be here"—Jessica gestured toward the platters—"in case you want another pie."

"I just might." Kip strode off with a wave, working his way through the crowd.

Suddenly, Jessica clutched Kaylee's arm. "I think something's wrong."

Kaylee glanced up to see the biplane still rolling down the runway. "Shouldn't he have stopped by now?" The planes always braked to stay within a certain area on the tarmac.

"That's what I thought." Jessica gnawed at her lip. "They're headed right for the bleachers."

The bleachers, where dozens of people sat.

"We've got a situation, ladies and gentlemen," Brett squawked over the intercom. "He's missed his mark and is still coming. People, get out of the way!"

17

With shrieks and screams, the seated spectators began streaming down off the bleachers. As the plane barreled along with no sign of slowing, collision appeared inevitable. People ran, some grabbing up children, others helping the elderly.

As the Waco E barreled along like a runaway train, horror held Kaylee in place, her limbs frozen. Jessica shielded both girls from the sight by holding them close to her sides. Around them, vendors and customers watched transfixed, whatever they were doing abandoned.

"Why doesn't he stop?" a man cried out.

A woman answered, "He probably can't. Something is wrong."

"Maybe the pilot passed out," another said.

Kaylee's eyes went wide at the idea. Had Wilfred had a heart attack or something? Then why didn't Reese take over?

Just when a collision seemed inevitable, the plane veered to the left, now heading toward a couple of hangars. Pained squawks came over the loudspeaker. "My plane," Brett moaned.

But another marvel of piloting occurred. The plane missed the buildings and instead crashed through a storm fence, the wooden pickets destroyed with a clatter, and finally rolled to a stop. The crowd erupted into cheers, sighs of relief, and tears.

Kaylee found herself running across the pavement, released from the paralysis that had gripped her. "I'm going to check," she called, the words lost to the wind. But over her shoulder, she glimpsed Jessica nodding in understanding.

She saw Brett burst out of the FBO, carrying a fire extinguisher. After that, Kaylee kept her gaze fixed on her destination, the yellow airplane sitting in the field. With what little breath she had, she whispered, "Please let them be okay." She chugged along, her legs like lead, one foot after another.

Brett passed her, breathing heavily as he lugged the heavy extinguisher. Another man flashed by: Kip Bates. Of course, he must be the most anxious of all about Wilfred's well-being.

Kaylee had reached the border of the runway when the airplane door opened. A moment later, Wilfred climbed out and slid to the ground. On the other side, Reese did the same. They both waved to the crowd to let them know they were okay. Kaylee heard cheers and shouts from behind her. She nearly collapsed in relief, but forced herself to keep going. Now that she knew they weren't hurt, she had to know—what had happened?

Kaylee clearly saw the moment Wilfred realized his son was there when a dumbstruck expression overtook his face. The two men stared at each other, and then Kip closed the distance between them and wrapped his arms tightly around his father.

Brett arrived, and Wilfred was introducing his son when Kaylee joined them. "Kaylee," Wilfred said, excitement in his voice. He took Kip's arm. "I want you to meet my son, Kip."

Kaylee said hello, not revealing that she was responsible for asking Kip to come. He went along with that omission, merely saying, "Hello, Kaylee."

Reese had come around the side of the plane so Wilfred introduced him as "my intrepid copilot, Reese Holt."

Brett was still holding the fire extinguisher, staring at the plane as if he expected it to burst into flames.

"You won't need that," Wilfred said. "Plane should be fine." He turned to the nose and winced. "Well, once you get the paint fixed." The fence had scratched the undercarriage when the plane trampled it.

Brett dropped the extinguisher with a clunk. "What happened?

Why didn't you stop?" Staring at the damage, he ran both hands through his curly hair, making it stand on end.

"The brakes didn't work," Wilfred said.

Reese had come around the side to join them. "Well, they did. Until they didn't." He pressed his lips together in a grim smile. "They failed halfway down the runway."

Brett let out a loud squawk of protest. "I can't believe it. This plane is perfectly maintained, regardless of the cost."

"And we didn't see anything when we did the preflight," Wilfred said. "Everything was fine then. Or appeared to be."

This news hit Kaylee squarely in the chest. Had someone tampered with the brakes? The person with the easiest access would have been the plane's owner. But why would Brett risk his precious airplane to hurt Wilfred? That didn't make sense.

Wilfred put his hand up to stop Brett from saying anything more. "Hold on. We've got company."

Kaylee glanced behind her and saw cameras and phones pointed their way, operated by reporters, including Jocko, and various onlookers. In this day and age, everyone had the ability to film events. One woman, standing in front of a camera with the plane in the background, was talking into a microphone, "Tragedy at the Turtle Cove Airport was averted today when pilot Wilfred Bates . . ."

Kaylee was sure the story and videos would go viral. She was thankful it would be because Wilfred and Reese had prevented a tragedy, rather than it being a lurid tale of untimely injuries or, heaven forbid, deaths.

Deputy Brooks pushed through the crowd, which was growing as people realized it was safe to approach the accident scene. "Step aside. Move out of the way, please." He drew an imaginary line with his foot. "Everyone behind this line." He pointed at Jocko, who'd continued to inch forward. "Including the press."

Jocko obediently retreated behind the line.

"Deputy," Kaylee said when he reached her. "How'd you get here so fast?"

Alan rested his hands on his duty belt. "I've been posted here all day. Our presence is required at large public gatherings."

"I'm glad." Kaylee wanted to voice her theory about sabotage, but now wasn't the time with the press listening in.

At the fringe of the throng a familiar, strident voice shouted, "Let me through. Move aside, I say!" Lorraine was pushing through the crowd, resorting to shoves when they didn't move fast enough. As usual, her son was trailing behind, benefiting from the path his mother forged.

At last Lorraine arrived in front of Wilfred. She struck a dramatic pose, one hand on her chest. "Wilfred. Honey. I about died when I saw you crash."

Wilfred's cheeks reddened and he shuffled his feet. "I'm all right, Lorraine. It was just a little bump against a fence."

Floyd rushed up to Wilfred and gave him a big hug. "I'm so glad you're okay."

Wilfred gently detached from Floyd's clumsy embrace with a back pat or two. "Thanks, son. All's well that ends well."

Not to be outdone, Lorraine nudged her son aside and gave Wilfred a hug too. "You're too modest." Hanging on to one of his arms, she addressed the reporters. "He's a hero, isn't he? Like that pilot who crash-landed in the Hudson River."

The reporters of course ate this up, snapping shots of the couple while snickering at Lorraine's over-the-top drama. Lorraine beamed back, clinging to Wilfred and generally acting like a smitten schoolgirl. Floyd lingered nearby, his eyes never leaving his mother and Wilfred.

After Lorraine's antics went on for a few minutes, Alan finally stepped in. "You're going to have to excuse us, ma'am. I've got department business to take care of."

Lorraine tilted her head with a smile. "But of course, Deputy. Don't let me interfere." She struck a coy pose, one eye on the reporters.

Brooks motioned Wilfred, Reese, and Brett to a distance away, then conferred with them quietly, to the crowd's consternation and disappointment. One reporter yelled out, "Statement!" and others soon added their voices to the demand.

Lorraine and Floyd joined Kaylee and Kip, who were standing to one side, waiting. Lorraine's mouth dropped open as she stared at Wilfred's son. "Kip? I didn't know you were back." Her tone was wary, her stance guarded as if she was afraid of his reaction.

Floyd nodded a greeting but kept his distance.

"I arrived this morning." Kip in turn sounded terse. He kept his gaze on his father and the other men. "How are you, Lorraine? Floyd?"

Caught up in the familial tension, Kaylee felt awkward, but curiosity compelled her to stay and talk to Reese about what had happened once he was done talking to the deputy.

"Oh, I'm fine." Lorraine's giggle was strained. "Floyd and I are busier than ever. Aren't we, Floyd? With our cleaning business, I mean. Deep Green, it's called."

"Glad to hear it." Kip folded his arms, making it clear that he wasn't interested in a protracted conversation with the woman his father was dating or her offspring.

After attempting to catch Wilfred's eye again a few times and failing, Lorraine said, "Well, we'd better get back to work. I was right in the middle of cleaning the FBO restrooms when my darling Wilfred almost died." With a sniff, she marched away, not waiting for a response. Floyd trudged along behind her.

"That was awkward," Kip said, echoing Kaylee's thoughts. "Sorry about that."

"Hey, none of my business," Kaylee said, although she was curious about the backstory that was clearly there. Why did Kip resent Lorraine? Surely he wasn't petty enough to care about his father having companionship. "I'm just glad you decided to come to the island."

"Me too." Arms still folded, Kip gazed around him, taking in the scene. "I'd have hated to hear about this on the news. Dad's an excellent pilot, but sometimes things happen."

Or they're made to happen. Kaylee didn't mention her theory about tampering. That suspicion needed to stay with the sheriff's department for now. *Jessica.* How could she forget to update her friend? Kaylee retrieved her phone from her pocket and called Jessica. "Everything is okay, Jess. Well, the plane is a little banged up, but Wilfred and Reese are fine."

"What happened?" Jessica's tone was laced with worry. "That was so scary."

"We don't know yet." Kaylee lowered her voice. "I'd like to hang around and see what I can find out. But I hate to leave you on your own at the booth, and with the girls too."

"I'm fine here. DeeDee texted that she's on her way. And I think it'll be a bit before people are ready to shop again."

"Okay. I'll come back as soon as I can." Kaylee returned her phone to her pocket.

Alan finally stood back, nodding at Wilfred, and the pilot moved toward the waiting crowd. "We'll give you a statement," he called out, "and then you're going to need to clear the area."

"That's right," Brett said. "We've got other planes scheduled to land and you're blocking the runway."

"Are you going to continue with the show?" someone asked. "Or is it canceled?" Groans and complaints met this question.

After another quick conference with the deputy, Brett said, "We will continue the show and the Apple Fest. This was an unfortunate freak accident." He tilted his chin toward Wilfred. "The pilot in command will give his statement now."

Wilfred squared his shoulders and cleared his throat, which quieted the last few whispers. He gave a brief summary of events, calling the incident "mechanical issues" that would be identified once an airplane mechanic examined the plane.

"Good save," someone called out.

"Better a fence than families," someone else said.

The audience burst into applause for Wilfred's masterful piloting.

"Thank you," Wilfred said, red staining his cheekbones. "My copilot, Reese Holt, was a great help during the crisis."

"Well, I am rethinking my decision to become a pilot," Reese quipped, to laughter and applause.

Brett stepped forward. "I'm Brett Horne, the airport manager. There is no reason to suppose that this one-in-a-million accident will happen again today. So we'll continue with the show on the hour." He stepped aside and pulled out his phone. A few moments later, another voice came over the loudspeakers, repeating Brett's words. The bystanders began to drift away toward the booth area, although no one returned to the bleachers, Kaylee noticed. She didn't blame them.

"Let's chat over in the FBO," Alan said. "Do you have a place that's private, Mr. Horne?"

"Sure. You can use my office." Brett began tapping on his phone again. "Head on over. I've got to get my plane towed to my hangar, then I'll join you."

As the group headed toward the FBO, Kaylee ended up walking beside Reese. "That was one of the scariest things I ever saw," she told him. Unable to help herself, she reached out and grasped his hand. "I was petrified."

"Me too," he admitted, squeezing in return. "But when you're flying, you can't give in to panic. Wilfred and I talked through the options, and crashing into that fence was the best one."

"I'm so glad you're all right. Not to mention those poor people on the bleachers."

"Me too." Reese glanced over to the now-empty seats. "I'll bet they won't put those there again. They were only put up for the air show, probably with the idea that having the plane come toward you when it lands would be thrilling."

Kaylee shuddered. "A little too thrilling."

While the men continued to the FBO, Kaylee detoured to the booth and grabbed a selection of Jessica's baked goods and tall paper cups of coffee. Reese and Wilfred needed a snack after their ordeal, and she knew Alan appreciated Jessica's baking—perhaps if she brought him a treat, he'd let her sit in on the questioning.

As she made her way to the main building to join the men, Kaylee mulled over what could possibly have led to the Waco E's mishap—and which of the people associated with the airport may have had a hand in it.

The web of connections extended beyond the island to when many of the players had lived on the mainland. Brett, Pamela, David, Don, Brett's father—they'd been connected while living in Seattle. Wilfred was a lifelong Orcas Island resident, so perhaps he hadn't known them well before they moved to the area. She really ought to ask him about it.

Floyd and Lorraine seemed to tie both groups together. They cleaned for Don, and Lorraine was dating Wilfred. Kaylee wondered how long they had been living on the island and made a mental note to find out. Kip also lived on the mainland, and he'd spent time in Seattle. Maybe he knew something that would shed light on this group of people.

Once inside the FBO, Kaylee glanced around, noting that the main room was deserted except for a woman seated at one of the tables shuffling through papers. As for Lorraine and Floyd, the only sign of their presence was *Wet Floor* signs near the restrooms. When the woman turned around, she saw it was Pamela Smythe.

"Hi, Pamela," Kaylee said. "I'm looking for Wilfred and Reese."

"Me too." Pamela laughed as she patted a stray strand of hair into place. "Wilfred, I mean. But Lorraine told me before she left that they're in a meeting." She pointed to a closed door. "In Brett's office."

"Thanks. I'll tell him you want to see him." Still holding the tray, Kaylee knocked.

Reese opened the door and stepped back to let her in. Wilfred, Kip, and the deputy were the only ones in the room, seated around a small conference table. Brett must have still been busy.

"Did Jessica make those?" Alan asked, his eyes lighting up. At Kaylee's nod, he gestured for her to enter the room. "Come on in. While you're here, maybe you can lend some insight."

Kaylee set the tray on the table and slid into a chair. The men reached for coffee and the baked goods, setting them on napkins she'd thought to bring.

Holding a turnover in his left hand, Alan flicked through screens on his tablet with the other. "So, who owns the plane?"

"Brett Horne," Wilfred said. "He asked me to fly it for him."

The deputy's head went up at that news. "Asked you to fly it? Why?"

Wilfred shrugged. "He said he wasn't feeling well. A stomach ailment. So I agreed to take her up and do some tricks."

"He asked me to come along," Reese said. "Under the terms of his bail agreement."

At the words "bail agreement," Kip lurched in his chair. His mouth dropped open before he closed it again with a shake of his head. Perhaps the fact of his father's arrest for murder was finally hitting home.

"He has to have another pilot on board at all times," Reese continued, "and his flight area is restricted."

"That's right," Wilfred said. "San Juan County only." He motioned toward Kaylee. "That's why Kaylee and DeeDee had to go visit Don for me."

"Don Heaton?" the deputy asked. Kaylee nodded and he held up a hand. "Interesting, but let's not get sidetracked. So the two of you went up in the plane at Horne's request. Did you notice anything wrong with it before you went up? Or something out of place, anyone lurking around?"

"No to all those questions," Wilfred said. "We did the usual preflight check, and I glanced through the logbook to make sure Brett was up to date with inspections. Not that I thought he wouldn't be. Any pilot worth his or her salt maintains their airplane. Otherwise . . . well, you saw what happened today. That would be way more common."

Brooks munched on his apple turnover while he absorbed this. "Okay. So there wasn't anything visibly wrong. How about in the air? Did everything seem okay up there?"

Wilfred and Reese exchanged glances. "The plane flew fine, the gauges worked, as did the rudder and ailerons," Reese said. "The engine sounded perfect."

"The problem happened when we landed," Wilfred said. "The brakes failed while we were partway down the runway, before we completely slowed down."

"That must have been really scary," Kip said, the first time he'd made a comment.

Wilfred's mouth quirked. "You might say we felt a slight prickle of alarm. And the runway is lined with obstacles. Not only people everywhere today, but hangars and those infernal bleachers."

Without glancing up from his note-taking, Alan asked, "So

what do you think happened?"

Again, the pilots exchanged glances. "I wouldn't want to guess," Wilfred said. "I think we should wait for the mechanic to take a peek. And the FAA will also be investigating, no doubt. We'll need to file an incident report."

Kaylee knew his approach was prudent but she found herself saying, "I think it was sabotage—and either Wilfred or Brett was the target." Under their questioning eyes, she clarified, "Brett asked Wilfred to take the plane up, right? I don't think he'd risk his own plane like that, but you never know. So maybe whoever tampered with the brakes expected Brett to be flying."

The deputy's eyes narrowed. "Why would someone want to try and hurt Brett Horne?"

"Or me," Wilfred added with a chuckle. "Of course, if someone thinks I killed David and wanted revenge—"

"Or thinks it will close the case if you meet with a fatal accident." Kaylee raised both hands. "I have no idea what happened. And I could be wrong. Maybe it *was* mechanical failure."

The gloomy expressions around the table told her that they doubted that explanation as well. After a moment, the deputy said, "I guess we'll wait for the mechanic's report before we take the next step. In the meantime, be careful."

"Always." Wilfred stood, his chair scraping back. "I'd better go call my insurance company."

Amid the hubbub of the others getting ready to exit, Kaylee reached out a hand to stop Wilfred. "Wilfred, on the way in here I ran into Pamela. She was looking for you."

He groaned. "I bet she is. Wants to take up where her husband left off, nag me into selling my farm."

Or force you to, using the loan as leverage. Kaylee's heart sank. Obviously David's demise hadn't removed the threat to the farm's future.

Kip's brow creased. "Want me to tell her to buzz off?"

"No, no," Wilfred grumbled. He pushed his chair into place, under the table. "I'll talk to her."

"If you say so." Kip pulled out his phone and began to check messages.

The trio left the room on the heels of Reese and Alan, who were chatting. Pamela must have seen the door open, because she was hovering nearby, an eager expression on her face.

"Wilfred," she said. "There you are. I want—" A dinging sound interrupted and she glanced down at the phone in her hand. She gasped, then held the phone out with a shaking hand. "Someone just threatened to kill me."

18

Deputy Brooks held out a hand for the phone. "Let me see that, ma'am."

Kaylee glanced over his arm at the screen and was able to read the text. *Back off if you don't want to end up like your husband.* That was pretty clear. What was the sender referring to, though? Trying to buy Wilfred's land was the simple answer—but nothing was simple about this case, Kaylee was coming to realize.

"Do you recognize this number?" Brooks asked. He held the phone so Pamela could study the digits. Kaylee did her best to commit them to memory herself.

Pamela shook her head. "No. I don't. But that's not surprising, is it?" Her smile was humorless. "I doubt a killer would provide identifying information."

Kip's fidgeting at the back of the group caught Kaylee's attention. Did he know something? She remembered he'd been playing with his phone only moments earlier. Had he sent the text? She sure hoped not, since that was a crime. But she resolved to find out his cell phone number when she got a chance. She only had a landline for him at the moment.

"Would you like to file a report?" Alan asked Pamela.

Pamela drew herself up, managing to rise another inch or so on her boot heels. "I certainly would. Whoever goes around threatening a poor widow needs to be sent to jail." She sniffed and tossed her head.

Since Pamela was still on Kaylee's suspect list, she regarded her distress with a touch of skepticism. Maybe she'd sent herself the text, to divert suspicion. It was an odd coincidence that it had come in while there was a deputy on the premises.

Brett Horne burst through the FBO door, a man on a mission. "Got my plane into the hangar," he said to the room at large. "The mechanic is checking everything over now."

"Good," Wilfred said. "I'd sure like to know what happened."

"You and me both." Brett leveled a baleful look around the circle, not even sparing Pamela. "We're going to have to postpone our meeting," he said to her.

She fluttered a bit. "That's understandable. Naturally, an accident is your priority. Just like this is mine." She snatched the phone from Brooks and thrust it into Brett's view. "Read that."

He mouthed the words as he read, brows rising as he went along. Something flickered in the depths of his eyes. "Huh. I wonder who sent that."

"Me too." Pamela pressed her lips together. "Someone is trying to scare me, but it's not going to work." This was a reversal of her earlier "poor me" act. She pivoted. "Wilfred, after I file my report, let's go grab lunch and talk. We have a lot to discuss."

He put up both hands and backed away. "Not today, Pamela. I've got business to take care of at the farm and here at the airport."

The two of them began to argue, speaking over each other with Kip interjecting comments. Deputy Brooks pulled out his whistle, ready to interrupt if need be.

Kaylee drew Reese aside. "I'd better get back to the booth. Please keep me posted with any updates about the accident."

"I will," he promised. "Want to have dinner later? I'll bring over takeout from Smokey Hauser's." A local barbecue restaurant owner, Jack Hauser, was offering mouthwatering smokehouse ribs and pulled pork at one of the vendor booths. Even the aroma drifting from his booth was incredible.

Kaylee pictured the two of them sitting on the porch at her cottage and enjoying a good meal. "That sounds wonderful." She sighed. "I could use a little relaxation right about now."

"We're on then." A mischievous expression crossed his handsome features. "Plus after dinner, we can practice."

Kaylee's eyebrows shot up. "Practice what?"

The mischief deepened into outright glee. "The other Petal Pushers didn't tell you? You four are singing backup for one of our songs."

"Wait, what?" Kaylee put a hand to her chest. "I'm *singing*? Oh, no way."

"Singing is only part of it. More like this." Reese gave a credible imitation of a finger-snapping, hip-swaying backup singer crooning nonsense words. The battling parties even stopped to watch, blessedly silent for a moment.

"I'm not getting on stage," Kaylee said. She turned on her heel and headed for the door. "Even if you do ply me with the best ribs in town."

"They're pretty special," Reese called after her. "They'll make you want to sing."

All the way across the grounds, Kaylee found herself snorting in disbelief at Reese's revelation. While many people dreamed of performing on stage, Kaylee was not one of them.

The only good thing about the situation was that it had taken her mind off the more serious concerns consuming her. Maybe Reese had done it on purpose, to make her laugh. That was it. It must have been a joke.

At the booth, Kaylee said to Jessica, "Reese told me the funniest thing earlier. He said we were performing with the Appleseeds."

Guilt crossed Jessica's face. "I didn't tell you?" She busied herself setting out a new tray of goodies, brought by DeeDee, who was unloading her car. "I thought I did. Or was Mary supposed to tell you?"

"Tell Kaylee what?" DeeDee asked as she approached the

booth with an armload of merchandise.

"Someone forgot to mention that we're performing tomorrow night." Kaylee pointed. "On that stage they're setting up over there."

"Oh yeah." DeeDee noticed Polly trying to carry a too-big armload of books. "Be careful, Polly. Zoe, will you help your sister?"

"You're awfully calm about this, DeeDee," Kaylee groused.

DeeDee swiveled to face Kaylee, her eyes puzzled. "I'm sorry. I thought it would be fun. I used to perform in musicals all the time."

"Me too," Jessica said. "And with the outfits Mary's putting together, it will really be a blast from the past."

The idea of appearing in public wearing a "blast from the past" outfit made Kaylee groan. "No, don't tell me. We're going to dress like go-go dancers."

Jessica and DeeDee burst into giggles. "Not a chance," DeeDee said when she caught her breath. "We're wearing long, full skirts and matching tank tops."

"It's going to take more than ribs from Reese to convince me," Kaylee muttered.

Again, the other two exchanged glances. "Ribs from Smokey Hauser's?" Jessica elbowed DeeDee. "Maybe we should have held out."

"I know." DeeDee rolled her eyes. "I heard the words 'stage' and 'backup singer' and I caved. I've always wanted to perform with a rock band."

"Not me." Kaylee glanced at the time on her phone. "I'm going to head to the shop now, after I make a detour to use the high-powered microscope at the lab. I totally forgot about the silverpuff seeds I collected." The thought of the lab made her think of the milkshake left in Don's room and the medication now being tested. Dropping off the silverpuff results would give her an excuse to ask Nick if they'd learned anything from it.

"We'll see you soon," Jessica said, singing the words to the amusement of Zoe and Polly. She wiggled her fingers at Kaylee. "Don't forget to get your vocal chords warmed up."

Kaylee didn't dignify that with an answer. She clipped on Bear's leash, grabbed her tote, and said goodbye.

She was almost to the parking lot when she saw Kip Bates walking toward her. "Hi, Kip. Any news yet about the plane?"

"Not that I've heard. Dad is over at the hangar, watching the inspection." He held up a duffel bag. "I'm changing into more casual clothing so I can help out at the farm booth and give those teenagers a lunch break."

"That's nice." Kaylee's mind whirled with so many urgent thoughts, she didn't know where to begin. "Kip, you used to live in Seattle, right?"

He nodded. "I went to college there. Why?" Bear pulled forward to sniff at his shoes and Kip smiled at him. "Hey, boy. Aren't you a handsome one?"

Bear wiggled all over at the compliment.

His approval of her dog warmed Kaylee. "To answer your question, I've noticed something about the people who may be involved in—" She stopped. In what? How much should she tell him? After all, he was practically a stranger. For all she knew, he was behind the whole thing.

She peered into his face. This was Wilfred's son. It was clear to her that he loved his father. She decided to trust him. "I've noticed something about the people who may be involved in David Smythe's murder, the development here, and every other strange thing that's been happening." She paused to gauge his reaction. He appeared interested, so she continued. "They all came from Seattle, and some of them knew each other. David and Pamela Smythe. Brett. Lorraine and Floyd. Your dad's friend Don Heaton."

"That doesn't surprise me," he said. "That they know each other, I mean. Most of them were members of the Friday Night Flying Club. I was too."

Bells rang in Kaylee's mind as she remembered Don mentioning that Brett's father was part of the same flying club. "Can you help me, Kip? I want to learn more about Lon Horne and what happened to him."

He shifted the duffel to his other hand. "You think it has a bearing on what's happening now?"

"I have no idea," Kaylee said honestly. "But we need to follow every lead, no matter how tenuous."

"Let's talk later," Kip said. He swung his bag forward a little, as though pointing it. "Right now I've got to get to our booth."

"And I'm on my way to town." Kaylee pulled out her phone. "What's your cell number? I'll call you later." As he recited the digits, she realized that it wasn't the same number as Pamela's threatening text. That was one small mystery solved.

Unless he faked the number on the text to Pamela, Kaylee thought with an internal sigh. Stranger things had happened.

"Good afternoon, Aida," Kaylee said as she approached the receptionist's station. "Is Nick in?" She held out an envelope holding the latest lab results regarding the silverpuff seeds. The plant matter from Hemlock Island was identical to that found on David's clothing, as she'd suspected. *At least it's one question answered.*

"I'm afraid not, Kaylee." Aida took the envelope and placed it in the correct mail slot. "He was called to the airport." The usually lively receptionist was somber when she added, "That airplane that almost crashed? The mechanic said it was sabotaged."

Kaylee's heart thumped, followed by a wave of cold shock, forcing her to grip the countertop. Wilfred and Reese might have been hurt or even killed, along with a lot of other people. The reality of the near miss made her head swim.

"You need to sit down?" Aida asked, her blue eyes creasing with concern. "You look like you're about to fall over."

"I'm okay." Kaylee took several deep, deliberate breaths, focusing on calming her racing heart. "I thought something like that might have happened, but having it confirmed caught me by surprise."

"It could have been bad—really bad, according to Alan. He happened to be out there."

"So was I," Kaylee said. "I saw the whole thing." She found herself relaying an eyewitness account to a fascinated Aida. "I was so relieved when they finally managed to stop and both pilots were uninjured," she concluded.

"I can understand that," Aida said, releasing a large breath that she'd apparently been holding for a while. "What a terrible thing to see. And you couldn't do a thing to stop it."

That was the worst part, Kaylee realized—being a helpless bystander. Bad things kept happening, and it was a miracle no one else had died. For a moment, she wallowed in a sense of futility. Then she gritted her teeth. *No.* She was going to find out who was behind David's death and all these mishaps, and she was going to do it before another tragedy happened.

"You go, girl," Aida said, obviously reading her expression. "I know you and the deputies will figure it out."

"Thanks, Aida. I needed to hear that." Heartened, Kaylee took her leave and sped to the shop. Before the day was out, she'd meet with Kip and hopefully talk to Nick. In any event, she'd keep moving forward.

At The Flower Patch, Kaylee parked out front, a rare event.

But downtown was practically deserted—thanks to the Apple Fest, she guessed. She and Bear climbed the stairs to the wraparound porch, Kaylee pausing to check the window boxes and container gardens along the way. Everything seemed fine, although she would probably change out some of the plantings soon, now that Halloween and late autumn were approaching. She liked to create themed designs for every season and holiday.

Mary appeared at the door to the workroom when they entered with a jingle of bells. "Kaylee, I'm so glad to see you."

To Kaylee's surprise, her assistant raced over and gave her a huge hug.

"What's that for?" Kaylee asked, laughing. "It hasn't been that long since I've been in here. Or has it?"

Mary pulled back, still grasping Kaylee's upper arms, and smiled. "It's a relief to see that you're okay. I heard what happened out at the airport this morning, and frankly I've been sitting here fretting. Oh, I know I would have heard if something happened to you, but I couldn't help it."

Kaylee bit her lip. "I'm sorry. I should have called."

Mary let go of her and knelt to fuss over Bear. "That's okay. It must have been quite a scene out there."

"It was." Kaylee crossed the room to the counter, where she set down her tote. "The press was out in force already so they were all over the situation. The sheriff's department is investigating. And the FAA was notified, as they are after every incident, apparently."

Kaylee hadn't realized how regulated flying was, even at the recreational level, though she supposed it was a good thing. Licenses, logbooks, inspections, FAA rules . . . A vague thought teased in the back of her mind, but she couldn't quite grasp it.

Mary held up a treat for Bear, who performed a spectacular leap to take it from her. "I saw a couple of videos online, and

I've been checking the news sites every five minutes too. Any idea what happened?"

Kaylee collapsed onto a stool, letting one leg dangle. "Aida told me someone sabotaged the airplane." Her words fell like stones into a quiet pond.

"Oh my." Mary's face went pale. "Reese and Wilfred. They could have—"

"Please don't say it. I know." Kaylee turned her attention to the ledger, which listed floral consultation appointments and arrangements people ordered. The bookings were slim this week, but things picked up the next week. That suited Kaylee just fine. Between the Apple Fest and the murder investigation, her plate was plenty full.

Mary sighed deeply. "Well, thank goodness everyone is okay. Who on earth would do such a thing? And why?"

Kaylee pushed the ledger aside. "That's what we need to figure out. And quickly."

"I'm in the middle of an arrangement." Mary gestured toward the workroom. "Come tell me everything while I finish it."

Kaylee followed Mary into the workroom and, while occasionally handing her assistant tools or disleafing flower stems, she took her through the events of the past couple of days.

Mary picked up a tangled bundle of *Gypsophila paniculata* and gently separated the fragile stalks. "It's a big fat mess, isn't it? And I'm not talking about this baby's breath."

"It sure is." Kaylee shook her head. "Want a coffee? I'm going to make a pot." She was in a midafternoon energy slump, and the day was far from over.

"Sure, I'll take a cup," Mary said. "Then I'd better head out to the Apple Fest to give Jess a break."

In the kitchen, Kaylee spotted a pile of soft, pretty clothing draped over one of the chairs. She inspected the clothes more closely, discovering pink, blue, green, and gold gauze floral skirts with matching tops. A yelp escaped before she could bite her tongue.

Mary popped her head around the door casing. "Are you—oh, you found our outfits. What do you think?"

Kaylee held the green skirt up to her body, guessing it was the one Mary had picked for her to match her eyes. Going by their coloring, DeeDee would get the blue, Mary the pink, and Jessica the gold. "I think I'd better start practicing my do-re-mis."

After a cup of coffee, Mary left for the Apple Fest, taking along two buckets of sleeved bouquets she'd found time to create between customers. In contrast to her assistant's energy, Kaylee sat hunched over on the stool, sipping a second cup of coffee, her mind empty. She was deliberately not thinking about all the mysteries of the past few days, knowing that she couldn't force answers.

Answers would come. They always had. She needed to have faith.

After serving exactly three customers, Kaylee locked up at closing time. Reese had texted that he'd be at Wildflower Cottage at six, which gave her time to shower and change, plus throw together a green salad to go with the ribs and coleslaw he was bringing.

The cottage always looked especially cozy on an autumn evening, a welcome sight. While Bear ran around the yard barking at squirrels and dried leaves, Kaylee opened the house to allow fresh air to blow in. Then she took a long, luxurious shower and changed into jeans and a cozy sweater. It was warm enough to eat on the patio, so she set the table out there with bright pottery dishes, a pitcher of ice water, and plenty of napkins to combat the saucy ribs.

Reese arrived while she was tossing the salad, carrying a big paper sack that smelled fabulous. At least Bear thought so, as he jumped up on Reese's shins the moment he entered the house.

"Down, boy," Kaylee said. "Sorry, no ribs for you."

"Sorry, buddy," Reese said to the dog. "But I'm sure glad I don't have to share." He considered, then grinned at Kaylee. "Except with you."

"You'd better." Kaylee swatted his arm lightly. "Put everything on the patio table, okay? I hope you like eating outside." She located the gourmet dog treats she kept for special occasions and gave one to Bear. He carried it outside and plopped down under the table, where he could keep a close eye—and nose—on the proceedings.

Kaylee took the salad to the table, along with tongs and a couple of dressings. They served themselves and dug in.

The ribs were smoky, with the sauce providing a tangy accent. "Yum," Kaylee said, wiping her fingertips with a napkin. "These are fantastic."

Reese raised an eyebrow with a knowing grin. "Good enough to convince you to sing for the Appleseeds?"

Kaylee dropped her napkin and laughed. "All right, you win. I'll sing backup." It was only one song. She'd survive. "Besides, Mary made me the cutest skirt to wear."

"If only I'd known that was all it took," Reese teased. "By the way, you ladies are meeting for a rehearsal tomorrow morning at your shop." For the last day of the Apple Fest, the vendor fair was only open from noon to three.

"Good to know." Kaylee smiled. Her friends had been so certain she'd agree. And they were right. She couldn't think of a time she'd said no to them.

Evening deepened, and Kaylee lit candles in the middle of

the table. After they finished eating, she made decaf coffee and they sat chatting, Reese showing no inclination to hurry home. Accompanied by Bear's soft snores under the table, they talked about their work, updates from friends and family—Reese especially liked hearing what Kaylee's grandmother was up to—and life on the island. Anything but the sabotage of the Waco E or other troubling events.

Close to ten o'clock, Reese's phone beeped with a text. He picked it up and read it automatically, then cringed. "I wish I hadn't done that."

19

"**W**as it important?" Kaylee asked, her chest tightening. Reese's relaxed demeanor had dropped away, replaced by tension. "Who texted you?"

"Wilfred," Reese said. "But it's nothing to do with either of us directly. Apparently the FAA official thought something was strange about the Waco E. He said it had been reported stolen by the owner."

"Lon Horne?" Kaylee guessed, her pulse leaping.

"That's right. Brett's father." Reese's lips twisted in a rueful grimace. "Quite the inheritance."

"That sounds like insurance fraud," Kaylee said. "He filed a claim but still had the airplane." Kaylee wondered how that tied into the loss of his charter business, not to mention his bankruptcy. Was it a way to raise cash to survive before the bank could seize the plane? But then he'd killed himself . . .

"Exactly. Wilfred told me some stories about that. The plane is flown away to an unknown destination, then it's reported stolen."

"How did Brett come to have the plane, then?" Kaylee wondered out loud.

"He could have retrieved it after his dad passed away," Reese said. "Maybe he didn't know about the insurance money, or maybe he just didn't care."

Just then, Kaylee's phone chimed. She picked it up expecting to see the same news Reese had received. Instead it was a text from Kip. *Coffee with me tomorrow morning?* She wrote back immediately suggesting Death by Chocolate and a time.

Reese watched her with curiosity in his gaze.

"I'm setting up a meeting with Wilfred's son that will hopefully answer some questions," Kaylee explained. "And this latest news will be on the list, for certain."

At the café the next morning, Kaylee suggested to Kip that they sit outside with their coffee and croissants. This way Bear could sit with them and indulge one of his favorite pastimes, watching people walk by.

The fall morning was crisp and fresh, with dew sparkling on the petals of the blooms on the porch at The Flower Patch next door. Shortly that dew would form frost, and summer's bounty would go dormant.

They settled in chairs, the metal scraping against the pavement, and arranged their breakfast. "This place is a nice addition to the island," Kip said. He took a bite of croissant. "Good as anything I've ever eaten. Including in Paris."

"You'll have to tell Jess that," Kaylee said, pleased by his compliment. "Thanks for meeting with me. I have to admit I'm stumped. And I do want to help clear your dad."

Kip nodded, his eyes on the coffee he held. "I appreciate that. Being back here . . . well, it hasn't been as bad as I thought." His smile was lopsided. "Except for Dad being a murder suspect, I mean."

"Yeah, that." Kaylee sipped her coffee, which had a touch of cinnamon. "It was finding the rat poison on his property that really pointed the finger."

Kip rocked back in his chair. "Rat poison? Dad would never—"

"I know. It would mean losing his organic certification. So someone put it there. To frame him, I'm guessing."

"Wow." Kip's mouth opened in shock. "That is truly evil. Dad has never done anything but help people all his life. Even Floyd."

Kaylee's radar pinged. "How did he help Floyd?" She kept her tone gentle, having gathered that Kip harbored concerns about the presence of Lorraine and her son in Wilfred's life.

"My dad has always looked out for him, been kind when he didn't necessarily need to be. Floyd's smart enough, but he's a little out there, you might say. He operates by his own set of rules, many of which don't make sense."

Kaylee tried to apply that description to the shy young man but gave up. She didn't know him well enough to evaluate Kip's assessment. He did seem to care about Wilfred, which was a point in his favor.

Kip pressed his lips together. "Anyway, let's take a step back to when I first met the Swifts." He swirled his cup, watching the coffee circle. "You probably gathered that Dad and I had a falling-out. It was because I tried to warn him about Lorraine. Being an adult, he didn't take too kindly to me interfering."

Kaylee merely nodded, sensing that he would get to the meat of the story soon. Traffic was picking up on the street, and customers came and went from the café in a constant stream.

"Lorraine is the type of woman who"—Kip glanced around to make sure no one was in earshot—"is intent on finding a wealthy husband. I saw her in action with Lon Horne. And before that, there was someone else, a man who died shortly after she married him." Kip shook his head. "Who do you think funded Lorraine's businesses? By the way, she went back to Floyd's father's name after her second husband died. Swift. They got divorced years ago, when Floyd was quite small."

Kaylee absorbed this. If Kip believed Lorraine was a gold digger, then his distaste for her made sense. "She was close to Lon?"

"Yeah. After she edged Pamela out."

"Pamela Smythe?" Kaylee recoiled a little from the tangled,

unsavory mess Kip was revealing.

"Pamela Granger at the time. She and David were only married two, three years."

And not happy ones, Kaylee reflected with a wince. "So was Lorraine around when Lon died?"

"She was dating him. She discovered his body. Suicide, they said." A troubled expression crossed Kip's face. "I sympathize with how hard that must have been. But she was already chasing Dad before Lon passed. She and Dad met when Don Heaton had a cookout at his new island home."

"Let me guess," Kaylee said heavily, "after Lon's charter business folded, Lorraine was ready to move on."

Kip nodded firmly. "Exactly. His whole operation went down like a deck of cards after the FAA started digging around."

"Who knocked over the first card?" Kaylee asked.

"Anonymous tip." His lip curled. "But I always thought it was David. He wanted to buy into the business, but Lon said no."

"It's probably a good thing, if Lon wasn't operating correctly," Kaylee said. "I wouldn't want to be part owner of something like that."

"True." Kip nibbled on his croissant, thoughtful. "Though David is—was—one of those guys who didn't care so much about cutting corners. Smooth operator."

"Did Brett think David was responsible?" Kaylee asked. "He was part of your flying group, right?"

Kip regarded her for a long moment. "I see where you're going with this. You think Brett might have sought revenge on David?"

Now Kaylee glanced around. Bear's posture alerted her to a workman in overalls moving about the alley next to the café, so she lowered her voice. "The thought had crossed my mind. He had the opportunity, since David likely drank the tainted coffee at the airport. But now he's working with Pamela on the development, which would be awkward, I would think."

Kip's eyes were sad. "That's because you're a normal person, Kaylee. You can't say the same for David's killer."

"You're right. And we're going to find out who it is. We're almost there, I can feel it." Kaylee was speaking out of instinct. Kip's information had helped flesh out some of the players and their motivations, but she wasn't quite ready to wrap the case yet.

"Do wop, do wop, do wop." The Petal Pushers sang and swayed in the flower shop's front room, a fascinated Bear their only audience.

The song ended and Jessica leaped to turn off the background music emanating from her phone. "That's it, girls. We've got it."

"Do wop, do wop," DeeDee sang again, then giggled and said, "Tonight is going to be so much fun."

The butterflies in Kaylee's belly belied that theory, but surely she could make it through one song without too much trouble. Right?

Mary put a hand on Kaylee's arm. "Listen, I'll go to the Apple Fest this afternoon for the last vendor hours. I know you want some time to work on the books here."

Kaylee was touched by her assistant's thoughtfulness. Mary knew that Kaylee got itchy if too many days went by before she reconciled the accounts. "Are you sure? I can come out and help tear down."

"No, we'll handle it. There probably won't be many people there anyway, so we'll likely pack up early."

Giving a final "do wop," DeeDee snapped her fingers and spun around. "We'll see you tonight, Kaylee. I figure we'll sit together and eat after the performance, since the guys are going on second."

"Good idea," Kaylee said, putting a hand on her uneasy stomach. The buffet dinner for the end of the event didn't tempt her at the moment. "I don't think I'll be able to eat until this is over with anyway."

After a productive morning in the shop, Mary left for the festival, and Kaylee settled down to analyze the shop's activities. In addition to how much they'd brought in, she liked to see what people were buying and try to spot any trends she could capitalize on.

While Kaylee was browsing industry news, her subconscious continued to work on the puzzle of David's death, and two questions drifted into her mind. She picked up her phone and texted Kip. *Questions: how did Lon die, and what other businesses did Lorraine operate besides cleaning?*

Her phone rang as she set it down, and she snatched it up again, eager to hear Kip's answers, but it was Nick. "Hi," she said. "I stopped by the station yesterday. Did you get my package?"

"Sure did," the deputy said. "Thanks. Now we know for sure that David Smythe picked up those silverpuff seeds on Hemlock Island."

"Did you hear anything from the lab about the milkshake or the medication?"

"Not yet. They said tomorrow, but they've said that a few times already. They're really backed up right now, apparently."

"I'm sure." Kaylee was disappointed but knew Nick was doing all he could to push the process along. "Any news about the Waco E? I heard it was sabotaged."

"Yep. The mechanic figured that out. Now the feds are involved, since it has to do with aviation. It's doubtful Wilfred did it, I can tell you that much."

No, most pilots wouldn't tamper with a plane they plan to fly.

"This case just keeps getting more complicated, doesn't it?" Kaylee said. "I had an interesting talk with Kip Bates this morning, if you'd like to hear about it."

"Sure, go ahead."

She shared all she'd learned about the group of flying club friends. "I sent Kip a couple more questions a little bit ago," she concluded, telling him what they were. "I figure if we keep asking questions, we'll peel enough layers off to get to the truth."

Instead of chastising her for overstepping, Nick sounded resigned. "Be careful Kaylee, okay? If anything strange happens, you call me. Don't try to handle it yourself."

"Of course, Nick. Oh, and if you're in the mood for a laugh, come see my singing debut tonight at the Apple Fest." She gave him the details, and they disconnected.

Closing time was approaching, so Kaylee cleaned up the counter area and got ready to lock up before stopping at home to shower and dress for the performance. She gathered Bear and her costume and left the shop.

Her phone dinged with a text while she was climbing into her SUV. She settled Bear, then read the text, which was from Kip. *Can you meet me at the farm? Have info to share!*

Will do, she wrote back, thinking that he wanted to answer her questions in person. If she hurried, she could stop at the farm and still make it to the performance on time. The Petal Pushers' number was halfway through the Appleseeds' set.

Kaylee sped toward home, grateful that the whole world seemed to be at the Apple Fest, so no one was on the roads. At the cottage, she fed Bear, realizing that she'd better not take him with her. "I'm sorry, boy," she said. "But I'll be gone most of the evening."

He whined, then shoved his face into his kibble as if prepared to eat his feelings. Kaylee gave him another pat and went to shower and change. Instead of her usual big purse, she packed a tiny bag with only the essentials—keys, lipstick, tiny perfume spray, and her phone. She thought about changing into her performance outfit, but in the end she decided it should wait until she got to the airport so it wouldn't get wrinkled or stained somehow. Carrying her clutch, a shawl, and a hanger holding the skirt and top, she said goodbye to Bear and headed for the orchard.

The farmyard was quiet, with only a couple of vehicles parked near the house. Kaylee chose a spot near the back door, figuring that Kip would be inside. Before getting out, she sent Mary a text to let her know where she was. She didn't want her friends to think she'd ducked out on them.

No one answered her knock. Thinking Kip hadn't heard her, Kaylee pulled out her phone to send him a text, smiling at doing so. *When did texting people on the same property become a thing?*

She couldn't find Kip's most recent text so she addressed the message by typing in his number. *I'm here.*

The answer came back a minute later. *Great. See you in a few.* Another text, *Oh, it was Bugging Out Pest Control.*

Interesting. He'd decided to answer one of her questions. But no one came to the door. Thinking Kip might be in the packing shed, where a light burned, Kaylee crunched across the gravel to the entrance.

The hum from the generators that powered the walk-in coolers was loud enough to be heard outside, so Kaylee didn't bother to knock before walking in. "Kip?" she called. The large main room appeared deserted, the conveyor belts shut down for the night. The fresh odor of organic-approved cleanser wafted on the cool air.

Something struck Kaylee in the back of the head. She cried out and fell to her knees, banging them on the concrete floor. Then everything went dark.

20

A rocking motion woke Kaylee. She kept her eyes shut, allowing the movement to soothe her aching head and body. Sleep sounded good right now, so good. Another minute and she'd be—

Hold on. Her head *hurt.* The packing shed. Someone had hit her.

Kaylee's eyes flew open, but she couldn't see a thing. Wherever she was, it was pitch-dark. Stuffy too, with a slight odor of mildew underlying a familiar citrus scent. She reached her hands out gingerly, afraid to either bang her knuckles or touch something unpleasant. On one side was a plastic wall, the other, only empty air. She was lying on something soft.

Water lapped and a gull keened. She was on a boat, perhaps in the sleeping berth. Moving slowly, her head pounding, she sat up and swung her feet to the floor. Her head was swimming but after a minute, it settled down.

Her eyes were adjusting to the dim light and she could see the outline of a door straight ahead. The string of her bag was biting into her neck. Thankful she still had it, she patted the contents and quickly realized her phone was missing. *Of course.*

Kaylee stood, shuffled forward, and hit her shins on something. A cardboard box with open flaps. When she put her nose closer, she smelled that distinctive citrus scent again.

The truth rang like a bell. She was on Deep Green Cleaning's boat, the one they used to travel to clients on other islands. Floyd or Lorraine—or both—were behind her kidnapping. And David's murder.

Pieces started clicking together in her aching head, but she didn't have time to stop and focus. She had to get out of there, fast. Her hand reached for the door handle. Expecting it to be locked, she stumbled when it opened toward her.

She froze, afraid her bold move might have been noticed. But nothing happened. All was silent, except for water and gulls, and somewhere nearby, the arguing voices of a man and a woman.

She stood in the doorway and peeked around the doorframe. Lit by a row of porthole windows, the main cabin stretched before her. The sizable room was lined with cushioned seats and stacked with cleaning supplies and tools. A galley and built-in table were at one end.

The bag strap was still uncomfortable and as she adjusted it, she got an idea. The vial of spray perfume fit perfectly in her hand. It wouldn't buy her much time, but it was better than nothing.

Kaylee stepped out into the cabin, holding onto the doorframe. She was still wobbly and weak. A few more steps and she reached a window. Although evening had fallen, she could see a light beaming down.

They were at a dock. Relief from a half-acknowledged fear swept through her. She'd been afraid that they were at sea, far from help.

If she could get onto the deck, she could make a break for it. Through the dim light on the galley stove, she perceived two exits—narrow, ladder-like staircases leading to doors at the front and back of the cabin.

The voices were coming from the front of the boat, the bow. She tread softly to the forward staircase and listened.

"I just can't believe you, Floyd." Lorraine's shrill squawk was easily identified. "What on earth are we going to do with her?"

A chill swept over Kaylee as the words sank in. They meant *her*.

"I don't know, Mama. Pitch her overboard? She's onto us, I tell you. I heard her talking to Kip."

The workman in overalls in the alley next to Death by Chocolate must have been Floyd. How had she not recognized him?

"What is wrong with you?" Lorraine's voice rose to a shout. "First you get my fiancé implicated in murder—"

Fiancé? *Ha, not likely.* Kaylee moved up a couple rungs to make sure she didn't miss anything.

"I didn't mean to, Mama. But his thermos was identical—"

So Floyd had swapped the thermoses. That was why Wilfred's fingerprint was on the one holding the poisoned coffee. It had been his thermos, not David's.

"That was bad enough, but the poison?" Lorraine growled in anger. "You had to hide it on his property?"

Although she couldn't actually see him, Kaylee sensed Floyd cringing. "I know, it was supposed to be temporary. But in all the excitement, I kind of forgot—"

"You'd forget your head if it wasn't attached. I had to fix your mistake by putting a box of poison in Pam and David's house."

"I'm doing my best," he whined. "After you told me about the loan paperwork, I got rid of it. And when you said that didn't matter, since Don knew about it, I tried to take care of him. But somehow the old coot survived. Both times, the medication and the milkshake."

A shiver ran down Kaylee's spine. Floyd had tried to kill Don too.

"That's because you're a screwup," Lorraine said. "David dying must have been a fluke." Her nasty laugh floated down the hallway. "Get your act together and go check on Kaylee. Make sure she's still sleeping. If not, you know what to do."

Kaylee ran, her head throbbing with each footfall. She considered going back into the cabin and feigning sleep but decided that wasn't a good idea. Floyd might hit her on the head again. No, she should get off the boat while she still had the chance.

Her pulse racing, she reached the stern ladder and began to climb, doing her best not to scrape her shoes on the wood. She had only a minute or so to get high enough that Floyd couldn't see her. And once he found her gone, he'd be after her in a flash.

Floyd's grunts told her he was climbing down the other ladder. She heard his heavy breathing as he rushed toward the sleeping berth.

"Floyd!" Lorraine's shout echoed in the main cabin. "Get back up here. We've got company."

The sound of his panting and thudding steps receded, indicating that Floyd had gone back toward the bow. Kaylee hung from the ladder, her arms and legs limp with relief. She was safe for now.

Then Lorraine's words sank into her terrified mind. Company? Had the deputies tracked her down? It had to be well past seven o'clock, so maybe someone was looking for her.

Kaylee clambered up the rest of the rungs, eager to reach the deck. But caution slowed her at the top. She didn't know for certain who else was on the boat, although she heard additional voices. She eased her head through the opening and saw—nothing.

A bulkhead was blocking her view. She climbed out, ending up on all fours. Not a bad position, even if it did awaken the bruises on her knees. She crawled along the deck and peered around the corner.

Brett Horne and Pamela Smythe. She almost cried out for them to help her, but then she heard Pamela snarling, "I figured it out, you little creep. You stole my logbooks so I couldn't sell my plane."

"And sabotaged mine," Brett said. "I'm going to have you arrested."

"I didn't do those things," Floyd protested. "Honest."

"You're the creep, Pamela," Lorraine said, a sneer in her

tone. "You tried to get Wilfred's organic certification revoked. Come on, admit it."

"What if I did? He killed my husband."

A silence fell. Brett spoke first. "Wilfred didn't do it. You two killed David, didn't you?"

"Not me." Lorraine threw her own son under the bus. "That's all on Floyd here."

Floyd glared at Pamela. "I got the idea from you."

Confusion was plain on Pamela's face. "Me? What are you talking about?"

In contrast, Floyd's expression was smug. "You killed Lon. With that rat poison I sold you. I bet it was in his hot chocolate. He sure did like his—"

"Shut up!" Pamela rushed at Floyd, slapping at his head and body.

"You killed my father?" Now Brett entered the fray, his body language displaying his internal struggle between wanting to attack Pamela and being reluctant to hurt a woman.

"I'm not saying a thing about that," Pamela said. "But now I get it. You stole my logbooks, didn't you? Trying to stop me from selling my plane."

"What if I did?" Brett said. "You never reported that prop strike. The thing's not safe."

"Says who?" Pamela barked. "And before you ask, I didn't touch your precious Waco E."

The pair glared at Lorraine, who backed away. As she turned toward the gangway, her eyes met Kaylee's.

Kaylee ducked back, but it was too late. Lorraine thundered along the deck in hot pursuit. Should she jump overboard, maybe? Or perhaps she could overpower the petite Lorraine . . .

As she mentally grasped for an escape, Kaylee clenched her fists and hope flooded her. The perfume was still in her hand.

She swiped her thumb over the top to make sure it was pointed the right way, then she stood and aimed.

The spray hit Lorraine squarely in the face. She screamed, throwing up both arms. "What was that?"

Kaylee didn't bother to answer. She sprinted to the rail and jumped. It was well past time to disembark.

She plunged into a frigid, briny bath of seawater. Thankful she was wearing lightweight clothing, she soon popped to the surface and began to swim, hiding in the dock's shadow. She didn't have much time before the cold water would numb her muscles and send her into hypothermia.

Up on deck, Lorraine shouted, "She jumped overboard!"

Pamela's voice was distinct. "Who?" Then the four criminals burst into excited babble, shouting orders and suggestions at each other.

A couple of slips down, a television flickered inside another boat. Urgency humming through her veins, feeling with every stroke as if she had a target on her back, Kaylee swam in that direction. At the neighboring boat's stern, she found the ladder and heaved herself up the rungs, water streaming from her clothing and hair.

Through glass sliding doors in the center cockpit, she saw a man with abundant gray hair smoking a pipe and watching the television. Kaylee ran on soggy sandals to the door, shivering as the water evaporated from her skin. She rapped on the glass, trying to be loud enough to alert him without giving away where she was to her captors.

The captain was so engrossed in the show, it took a moment for her knocking to get his attention. He swiveled around holding the pipe, amazement on his weathered features. Then he jumped up and threw open the door.

"What happened to you? Fall overboard?" He drew her

inside. "I'm Captain Sam. Let me get a blanket."

"No, there's no time for that." Kaylee's teeth began to chatter. "Call 911. I was kidnapped."

"Kidnapped?" His furry brows rose. "What on earth—"

The whirl of blue lights approaching the dock caught their attention. "I guess they already figured it out," Kaylee said, slumping onto a bench. "I will take that blanket now."

Several cruisers squealed to a halt, and deputies emerged, streaming toward the boat slips. Kaylee's rescuer went on deck and flagged down the officers. "I've got her, deputies. She's okay."

Nick Durham was in the lead. "I'd like to see proof of that, sir." Behind the cruisers, other cars pulled up, doors slamming.

Kaylee, feeling better now that she had the blanket, walked out on deck. "Here I am, Nick." She pointed to the Deep Green Cleaning boat, which had started and was maneuvering away from the slip. "Floyd Swift kidnapped me. Lorraine Swift, Brett Horne, and Pamela Smythe are also on board. I heard all of them confess to various crimes."

"Kaylee." Reese pounded along the deck, followed by Mary and the other Petal Pushers. "Are you all right?" A high-pitched barking echoed and Bear passed them all, jumping and leaping in a frenzy.

Nick was already on his radio ordering the marine patrol to intercept the Deep Green boat. Sam helped Kaylee off the boat and she scooped up her dog. "How did you all find me?" she asked.

"We saw your SUV in the parking lot while we were searching for you," Mary answered. "Floyd brought you here in your own vehicle. He left the Deep Green van at the farm."

"He's not the smartest of criminals, I guess," Deputy Brooks said.

"Smart enough to poison David Smythe and try to poison Don," Kaylee said. "Floyd and his mother were arguing about it. He stole the loan documents too, in a misguided effort to help Wilfred. Though he shouldn't have used Wilfred's thermos—that was dumb."

Nick had returned to the gathering and was taking notes. "What other crimes did you hear them confess to?"

Kaylee took a breath, thinking back to what she'd heard. "Well, I think Pamela might have poisoned Lon Horne. Floyd accused her of it. And Brett stole Pamela's logbooks. I'm pretty sure Lorraine sabotaged Brett's plane and almost killed Reese and Wilfred."

"And a whole lot of other people," DeeDee said.

"Nice gang," Herb muttered.

"We learned something else from the FAA official," Nick said. "Pamela's plane had an accident years ago. But that was never disclosed in the sales documents. So something fishy is going on there."

"That's right," Kaylee said. "The plane had a prop strike, whatever that means. I think Brett was planning to blackmail her. I wonder if Lon knew about it, and that's why she killed him."

"Like Herb said, nice gang," Luke Roberts commented. "And by the way, a prop strike is when the propeller hits the ground or another object." At the amazed looks from his friends, he shrugged and added, "I heard pilots talking at the Apple Fest."

Now that she'd shared the resolution of the murder and other crimes, Kaylee's thoughts latched onto another mystery. "How did you know something was wrong?"

Jessica pushed through the group to hug Kaylee, either oblivious or not caring that she was soaking wet. "Kip invited you to the farm to tell you about the prop strike. He was on his way to the farm when you texted him that you were there, but you were gone when he arrived. The cleaning van was there but you weren't, so he called us."

"Since you weren't at the farm, we checked your house." DeeDee took up the tale. "When you weren't there either, we put out the alarm. And we brought Bear along because we figured he could sniff you out anywhere."

"We knew the Swifts owned a boat," Alan said. "Mary and Herb found your SUV in the parking lot. And that was that."

"Thank you all." Kaylee's heart warmed with gratitude for her friends and their diligence in tracking her down. She told them how she'd escaped, then apologized for missing the Appleseeds' performance.

"Oh, you didn't miss it," Mary said. "When you didn't turn up, we asked to be bumped to a later slot."

"Seriously?" Kaylee wasn't sure whether to smile or groan.

Herb glanced at his watch. "And we'd better head back over right now."

Kaylee raised an eyebrow at Nick.

"Go on," the deputy said. "We'll catch up later." A grin creased his face. "And someone better film you actually getting up on stage. Or at least take a picture."

"You'll get to see it," Andy Wilcox said. "The whole event is being live-streamed on the chamber of commerce's social media page. I'm sure they'll post a recording too."

Kaylee groaned. "I wish you hadn't told me that." But to her surprise, the idea of performing didn't hold quite as much anxiety as it had previously. What she'd just been through put things into a bit of perspective.

"I'll drive you," Reese said. "It'll give you a little more recuperation time."

She gladly accepted his offer, thankful for his thoughtfulness. Captain Sam let her keep the blanket, and they all headed off to the airport.

Once they arrived, everyone else went to the stage area

while Kaylee entered the FBO, Bear sticking close to her side. The building was oddly quiet, she noticed, conscious that Brett Horne wasn't there. In fact, he might never return.

As she entered the women's room to change, Kaylee wondered how the marine patrol chase was going. Hopefully the criminals would surrender without incident.

Then she glimpsed herself in the mirror and gave a little shriek. Her makeup was gone and her hair was soaked, hanging in long strings around her shoulders. "This will be a challenge." Her gaze fell on the hand dryer. "We're in luck, Bear. Sort of."

The restroom door opened and Mary popped in. "I thought you might want some makeup." She opened her handbag and began to forage.

"Bless you, Mary," Kaylee said. "You read my mind."

Once she was ready to Mary's satisfaction, they hurried out of the FBO and across the tarmac toward the stage. The evening was warm and starlit, and Apple Fest attendees were milling about the barbecue tent or listening to a country-western act's encore.

"Thank you, ladies and gentleman," the lead singer said. "You've been a great audience. You'll enjoy the next group, who will be playing classic rock. Please welcome the Appleseeds!"

The audience clapped while one set of musicians exited the stage and the Appleseeds took their place. Mary whisked Kaylee up onto the platform so fast that she didn't have time to think about what was happening.

Then the first notes of a familiar song sounded. Kaylee, standing between Mary and DeeDee, found herself snapping her fingers and swaying. The other Petal Pushers joined in, moving as one, celebrating in song.

Up to this point, we've been doing all the writing. Now it's *your* turn!

Tell us what you think about this book, the characters, the bad guy, or anything else you'd like to share with us about this series. We can't wait to hear from *you!*

Log on to give us your feedback at:

https://www.surveymonkey.com/r/FlowerShopMysteries

Annie's® FICTION